The Starligh

Pale Stars in Her Eyes
The Covenant

Annabel Wolfe

EROTIC ROMANCE

Siren Publishing, Inc.
www.SirenPublishing.com

A SIREN PUBLISHING BOOK
IMPRINT: Erotic Romance

THE STARLIGHT CHRONICLES
Pale Stars in Her Eyes
The Covenant
Copyright © 2008 by Annabel Wolfe

ISBN-10: 1-60601-347-5
ISBN-13: 978-1-60601-347-2

First Printing: November 2008

Pale Stars in Her Eyes and The Covenant
Covers design by Jinger Heaston

All cover art and logo copyright © 2008 by Siren Publishing, Inc.

Printed in the U.S.A.

PUBLISHER
Siren Publishing, Inc.
www.SirenPublishing.com

PALE STARS I

The Starlight

Annabel

Chapter 1

The clothing was unfamiliar and Jerra realized with a swift glance in the mirror she had the damned thing on backwards. With a muttered expletive, she pulled the soft material back up over her head and turned it around before she slipped the gown back on.

Good God, that was even worse.

She stared at her reflection, seeing the crests of her areola visible over the clinging drape of the neckline. The other way, her breasts were minimally covered so she took it off once more. Her nude body gleamed in the light of the passing stars outside the window of her cubicle and the soft glow of a single recessed light. She put the gown back on the way she first had it and had to be satisfied with the fact the amount of skin showing was indecent. At least her nipples weren't exposed. After all, she had no choice but to wear it.

The door slid open behind her without warning and she whirled, grateful her visitor hadn't entered the moment before and caught her naked. Heat rose into her cheeks as the man who stood in the doorway deliberately raked her body with cool, appraising perusal before he gave a curt nod. He commanded, "Come with me."

"Where?" she asked, her hands clenched at her sides. The dress barely covered her upper thighs and she fought the urge to tug the gauzy material lower.

"It isn't your place to ask." In his uniform of tunic, fitted pants, and polished boots, Lieutenant Herad was an impressive figure. Taller than most human males, he filled the doorway to the room that had been her cell for the past few days. His features were starkly masculine, and his dark hair was immaculately neat, tied back from his angular face. He looked both stern and annoyed. "You've been schooled, Miss Aubrey."

"I've been kidnapped," she said bitterly, even though it was probably a stupid thing to argue when she was on a strange ship, bound for a destination unknown, with no protection or a single familiar face. "You took me from my home, violated my privacy in every way possible, and no one has explained to me why. Yes, I've been told to cooperate, to stay quiet and obedient, but forgive me if I'm not interested in pleasing my captors."

"You'll please at least some of us, don't worry, whether you want it or not. And you know full well we harvest females from Earth." His tone was cold and detached. "It is our legal right."

Jerra fought a shiver of apprehension. Yes, she knew the S-species were in domination and agreements had been made because there had been little choice. Her planet was defenseless against the evolution of a new form of life, the result of a colonization effort and incredible genetic advances. The S-species, or Superhumans, were physically and mentally superior in every way to her ordinary, original race. They were children of the old Earth, spawned to live in diverse conditions on distant planets.

Who would have guessed within a few short generations, they would rule most of the known galaxies and keep their mother planet neatly under their thumb with very little effort?

"What about my parents?"

"They've been compensated, don't worry. They knew this was coming, for they were informed last year we'd decided you were suitable."

They had known? In retrospect, she had noticed her mother or father hadn't been as affectionate in the past months, probably in sheer self-defense over her inevitable departure.

It was impossible to keep her voice from wobbling. "You intend to breed me?"

"Yes. Eventually." His gaze was steady and unapologetic though he must have caught the edge of fear in her voice. "Right now, we are headed out on a diplomatic mission that will take the better part of a year in your terms of time. On the return voyage to Minoa, you will be impregnated."

She felt a little dizzy at that revelation, though it was what she feared all along. The S-species were very careful not to become inbred and took human females to make sure the genetic pool did not narrow too much. Jerra said recklessly, "I wish I'd simply broken the law and not stayed a virgin."

"And had it discovered and been thrown in prison?" He lifted a dark eyebrow in reproof. "Come now, Miss Aubrey, we both know you are too intelligent for such a foolish decision. It's part of the reason you were chosen. According to the mandatory tests, you have a high level of cognitive function that's entirely natural. You also meet all the other standards—good health, a sense of self-preservation strong enough to obey the laws, and the most important, physical beauty."

Well, lucky me.

"That's why we have to take the tests as children?" she asked with cold fury. "So you can pick the next specimen to breed like an animal? We're told it is to monitor the evolutionary process of mankind."

"Humans don't need to know everything. Besides, you will not be bred like an animal, but like any woman, inseminated by a fertile male during sexual intercourse. In the meantime, however, the journey is a long one and the males get restless, even the most disciplined, without sexual activity. We learned a long time ago having a female available when the need arises helps the crew. You'll be most useful, I am sure."

The blood drained from her face. She could feel herself go pale. "You…you expect me to…to…with your entire crew?"

For the first time, he looked amused. "No, of course not. Do you have any idea how many soldiers and flight crew there are on a ship this size? Besides, we aren't barbarians, quite the opposite. I think you'll actually find your assignment both an honor and a pleasure. Now, come with me."

She doubted the part about feeling honored and even more the pleasure, but his assurances were a distinct relief. Her current predicament was bad enough. Jerra didn't move. "What assignment?"

A low sigh escaped him and his eyes narrowed. The lieutenant muttered, "What a stubborn female."

"We all fear the unknown. I imagine even the S-species has that problem. Just tell me and I am much more likely to cooperate."

"That would be refreshing, but trust me, you'll cooperate either way." He explained briskly, "You will share quarters with three males. Colonel Ian Helm who is in command of the military presence on this vessel, Larik Armada, who is a brilliant engineer, and maybe you've heard of Ran Kartel, the diplomat who leads this expedition. For the duration, you are theirs."

Though she normally did not follow interplanetary news, for there was enough in her own world to keep track of, she had heard of Kartel. He had negotiated several treaties that were thought impossible, and was reputed to have not only persuasive powers but physic abilities.

Three men?

The idea was daunting and mortifying. One moment, she had been living a normal life and now, she was supposed to be a concubine to three strangers who would use her only for physical pleasure. No wonder they'd given her clothing that barely covered her body.

This is insane…

But apparently it was real.

"Come," Lieutenant Herad said for the third time with no equivocation in his voice.

There didn't seem to be anything to do but obey.

* * * *

He felt her before he saw her.

Ran Kartel glanced up sharply, waiting for the door to open. The girl was apprehensive, and waves of uncertainty and dismay rolled like a lapping ocean surf through his mind. He wasn't sure he blamed her, for like all the human women on the ship, she had been plucked from her placid earthly existence and brought as a captive to please the men on board. All would later be bred to keep the bloodlines free of mutations and weaknesses in immune systems. To him, the practice was not entirely fair, for his government preached impartial rule, but he had not crafted the legislation that put it in place. Nor was he involved in any way in the harvesting program, except one.

He would reap the benefit of not having to go three months without sex. That length of time would be nearly impossible, for along with elevated intelligence and superior physical size was an increased sex drive among his kind.

"She's being brought in," he murmured to the other two men sitting at the table in the common area of their berth. The room was round, and each of them had a sleeping cubicle. On the other side was a different room, this one with a large window through which a bed was visible from the community area where they ate their meals.

The window into the room served two purposes. The first was so they could enjoy watching the girl at all times, even when they weren't using her. After all, she was there for their pleasure. The second was to show when she was with one of them, and already occupied.

It was quite a practical arrangement, for there was simply no way to bring a woman on board for every man. The soldiers had to share ten to one and schedule their time, but since he, Armada, and the colonel were the highest raking men on the ship next to the admiral, they were given not only the privilege of sharing between fewer men, but the most beautiful of the captives.

Armada, the engineer who designed the new super engine that now powered them with silent force across the depths of space, lifted his fine brows. He was like most S-species and remarkably good-looking. Thick fair hair waved around features that were both sculpted and classically handsome. He was tall, leanly built, and keen intelligence showed in his remarkably blue eyes, their color pure cobalt. He said, "I'm told she has blond hair and the color is actually real for a change with human women." He grinned, making his face look boyish. "Her snatch is just a slightly darker shade."

"How the hell do you know that?" Ian Helm gave him a glimmering look, his long fingers wrapped around the stem of his glass. He was a contrast to the young engineer with sleek dark hair, high cheekbones, and eyes dark as the endless universe without stars. He was known as a remarkably brave soldier, his build massive and heavily muscled, and he was a good six inches taller than either one of them even though they were considered tall males. Ran had always thought privately he wouldn't want to ever really see him angry, but normally, the colonel was a very controlled man and had an agile mind under pressure.

"Dr. Yent did the examination. He mentioned to me she was a gorgeous specimen of a human female and her hymen unbroken until he did it surgically. The blood tests confirmed she's entirely clean of any of their typical diseases."

"You would ask for such details." Helm looked amused. "Blood tests, purity issues, and the color of her pubic hair. Tell me, did you inquire on the state of her teeth?"

"I'm an engineer. We like to know just what we're dealing with. Details are important to us." Armada laughed.

"Soldiers are less complicated, I guess. I just don't want my dick to be best friends with my hand for the entire way to Septinium and back. A warm female, S-species or human, beats the hell out of masturbation any day. I'm already tense and we've been out only a few days."

"She's frightened and not particularly willing," Ran interjected. "I feel it."

Both of them looked at him, their expressions hard to read, but he felt their first reaction was one of surprise he even brought up the girl's feelings. After all, she was just a human and a captive at that. Larik said, "Surely she's been instructed our captives are never ill-used. Besides, at her intelligence level, she must realize she has no choice."

It was true, she didn't have a choice but to submit and service them whenever they wished. Still, Ran wasn't interested in a woman who didn't want sex as much as he did. "I just think we should approach this the right way. The four of us are stuck with each other this journey in close quarters, and as you pointed out, Colonel, it's a long one. If we take care to make sure she's sexually initiated with as much sensitivity as possible, she'll be much more likely to participate with enthusiasm."

"That's logical." Armada nodded thoughtfully, taking a sip of wine in his cup. "I want to be fucked back. I've never taken an unwilling woman, human or not."

Helm blew out his breath in a small sigh. "I guess I hadn't even thought about how the woman might feel. We're told it doesn't matter because the humans have no rights. I just knew she was going to be here with us for that purpose and my cock took over. I've never forced myself on any female who wasn't ready to spread her legs with enthusiasm."

Ran looked around the table. "Which one of us then, goes first? She's a virgin, though thank the stars and moons it won't hurt her because the medical procedure took care of the physical part of it. If properly aroused, she'll enjoy it even her first time."

Helm shook his dark head, his raven hair shifting across the material of his uniform. "I'm very big," he said with obvious reluctance. "Probably too big for an uninitiated woman. One of you two should probably break in our beautiful guest."

That revelation was not a surprise, considering how large the colonel was in every other way, his cock probably was huge. *And 'guest'*, Ran thought, *is the wrong word*. 'Slave' was more appropriate, but he refrained from mentioning it. He looked at Armada. "We can toss for the privilege."

The young engineer thought for a moment, and then said, "No, you do it, sir. You'll know just what she's feeling every moment and surely that'll help you guide her in the right direction. I can wait for her to adjust to the arrangement."

Maybe it was just as well they both agreed before the door slowly slid open. Lieutenant Herad stepped in first, saluted the colonel, and then turned and made an imperious motion with his hand. The creature who answered the unspoken order made the room fall to a sudden hushed silence as she entered.

The first thing that sprang to Ran's mind was that the rumors of her beauty were not exaggerated. Instead, they didn't do her justice. Shining golden hair tumbled over slim, tense shoulders, framing a perfect oval face. Her features were delicate and fine-boned with arched dark blond brows, a straight small nose, and a soft pink mouth. A flush stained her smooth cheeks as the silence lengthened and they stared at her. Long lashes dropped slightly over a pair of azure eyes, the color not the almost startling sapphire color of Armada's, but instead like the pale stones mined on his native planet, Minoa. Her body also rivaled any fantasy, male or female. The girl was slender and lissome, her arms and legs bare, and from what he could see of her breasts and the depth of the inviting cleft between them, her tits were spectacularly large and lush. She wore the standard issue for a female sexual slave—a scanty gown made of an almost sheer material that was a token covering but little more.

She didn't move or speak, not even when Herad nodded his head at their unspoken approval of his choice and silently left the room.

The door swished shut.

Armada finally tore his gaze away and muttered, "You lucky bastard, Kartel."

The girl heard the words and her gaze shifted to him. There was a hint of defiance there and Ran sensed it too, the willful urge to resist even though he knew she had been warned punishment would be involved if she didn't submit. It almost overrode her fear, but not quite, and the warring emotions crowded his mind.

He met those lovely blue eyes, holding her gaze deliberately. "I agree," he told his comrades, without looking away. "Very damned lucky. We all are. Now...if you will excuse me, I think I'll introduce myself."

Chapter 2

"This will be your room."

The declaration, spoken in a smooth, almost mesmerizing voice, made Jerra glance around. It was much larger than the tiny stateroom that had been her prison for the past days since her abduction. The floor was smooth but warm under bare feet, and there was literally no furniture, except a large bed set right in the center of the space. A small door was open to show a tiny cleansing room, but the most puzzling thing was a window, open to the room she had just come from. Through it, she could still see the other two men sitting at the table, sipping their wine and watching her. There was no window to the outside world, not even so she could see the monotonous slide of sparkling stars in the distance as they moved through space.

She looked back at the man who had taken her hand and led her inside. "Which one are you?"

"Kartel."

"Oh."

The famous diplomat was a tall man, but so far, all the S-species seemed to tower over her. His hair was a rich brown chestnut shade, with golden streaks here and there, and it waved against the strong column of his neck. His face had an elegant yet completely masculine beauty to it with clean lines to his nose and jaw, and a sensual mouth. Arched brows just slightly darker than his glossy hair emphasized his striking eyes. They were a beautiful deep verdant green that on an average human would look unnatural, but on him seemed to fit. Wide shoulders filled his tunic, his legs looked long and athletic, and his posture seemed utterly relaxed. His lips curved in a small smile as if he knew what impressions she was receiving.

Since the evolution, she'd heard the Superhumans were all extraordinarily good looking, and the three men she was to serve certainly fit the description. She supposed that fact was one small consolation.

He said, "You know why you're here."

It wasn't a question and she didn't treat it as one. "You don't waste any time, Ambassador. I've barely arrived. And here we are." She indicated the bed, hoping he didn't notice the trembling of her hand before she let it fall back to her side.

He laughed at the sarcasm in her tone, a low ringing sound that echoed in the chamber. "I see no use in waiting, for you'll only grow more apprehensive. All three of us are already restless and could use some activity to take off the edge, especially myself and Colonel Helm. There is precious little for us to do on the journey. Our job begins when we arrive at our destination."

"And I am to be your…entertainment in the meantime?" She lifted her chin as she spoke, though her heart pounded and her stomach felt tied in knots.

Softly, he said, "We will also entertain you. Tell me, what is your name?"

For a moment, she hesitated, but then she shrugged because she couldn't see the point in refusing, especially since Herad knew it anyway. As far as she could tell, her captors knew everything about her, inside and out. "Jerra Aubrey."

He inclined his head, and his green eyes seemed to look right through her. "There's no need to be afraid, Jerra. Your presence here is about sexual pleasure, nothing more."

"That's the trouble. Nothing more? I am an object to you, not a person, and this is not my choice."

"Certainly you can choose to make the best of what has happened to you. Maybe you didn't know this, but captives quickly flourish in our care. None I've heard of want to go back to their previous life, which should tell you something. Enjoy your time on this journey, and afterwards, breed children as beautiful as you are. You'll be nurtured and well-cared for by the most powerful beings in this universe."

The man was a diplomat, after all, and he specialized in soothing disgruntled rulers and irate nations. It was no wonder he thought he could cast her platitudes and soothe her into his bed, Jerra thought resentfully.

For there was no doubt that was why they were in the room. She didn't have any experience with men, but the way he looked at her indicated an intense carnal interest that was unmistakable.

He was going to have sex with her and there was nothing she could do about it.

"I won't resist you," she said coldly. "But I won't enjoy it, either."

"Are you so sure? You're a virgin after all and have no experience. Most females enjoy sexual release equally as much as men. I think you're going to be pleasantly surprised."

After her physical examination, she'd been taken with the other prisoners to a large room where they had been instructed on how to behave during their duties. There had been little to no explanation about what actually was going to happen, but instead emphasis on cooperation and obedience. Jerra looked at the tall man in front of her with a glimmer of uncertainty. He certainly seemed amused *and* sympathetic to her trepidations, which she had not expected.

"Let's find out, shall we?" He indicated the bed with a graceful movement of his long-fingered hand. "Take off your gown and lie down."

"With them watching?" She felt at once flushed, her heart pounding harder. All she knew about sex was what she'd read in books. Since she was below the age the government would give consent for her to marry, she wasn't allowed much around men on her home planet. A woman had to be twenty-five, and everyone understood it was because the S-species wanted to be able to pick and choose who they wanted.

"If they want to watch us, they can. That's why the window is there. Also, we can tell that way if you are already occupied."

Her cheeks flushed deeper. "Occupied?"

"This chamber is made just for the purpose we are about to use it for, Jerra. You'll also sleep here." He began to unfasten his tunic, his eyes taking on a glitter that made them more brilliant than ever. "Now, the gown, please."

He dwarfed her in size and could easily force her, so she grabbed the hem of the filmy garment and jerked it up off over her head. Without looking at him, her face averted in embarrassment over her nudity, she did as she was told and climbed into the middle of the bed. She felt very much on display, knowing all three of them could see every bare inch of her and fought the urge to try and cover herself with her hands.

It was easy to know when he followed, for the mattress dipped and she suddenly felt the warmth radiating from his skin as Kartel reclined next to her.

Naked.

Without thinking, she impulsively looked over out of sheer curiosity. He lay propped on one elbow, and a wickedly attractive smile hovered on his mouth. Her lips parted in surprise as she saw the hard, defined muscles of his chest and shoulders, the sinewy length of his legs, dusted with a light covering of hair, and most startling of all, the bold length of his engorged penis high against his flat stomach.

It looked very long and entirely too big to put inside her, and she studied his arousal in unwilling fascination. The smooth length had veins visible from base to the flared tip. A small hole crowned the crest, the slit shiny with droplets of fluid. She could see his shaft pulse slightly in a regular rhythm and realized with a small shock it was the steady beating of his heart.

"You're curious, aren't you?" he murmured. "And desirable as hell, which is an excellent combination in a bedmate. We'll all be happy to teach you every way you can please us. We'll also demonstrate exactly how we can please you."

Jerra had to force her gaze away from his straining erection. It frightened her, but she was also inexplicably intrigued. "Why would you care about pleasing me? I'm simply a warm convenient toy with the correct anatomy for you to use."

His smile widened. "How convenient for you that the portion of *my* anatomy I'll use is also a tool to bring you sexual satisfaction and great pleasure. And we do care about you being pleased in a selfish way, I suppose, for it enhances the experience for the male when the female enjoys intercourse. Tell me, did you receive an injection this morning?"

She had, though no one had bothered to tell her why. She nodded, doing her best to resist the urge to return to staring at his formidable erect cock.

"The shot was to enhance your sex drive and bring it up to an S-species level. You'll get them from time to time on our journey." He still hadn't touched her, but just looked at her with his captivating eyes, his voice smooth and unthreatening. "So you see, we are not interested in only your luscious body, but also your general well-being. The happier you are with us, Jerra, the more we can all enjoy each other."

Was it true? God, she hoped so for her situation had seemed so hopeless.

"I'm not lying, Jerra, and I'm glad your fears are easing a little."

Before she could speak, he moved. Nothing sudden, just a shifting of his weight so one sinewy thigh slid over hers, trapping both her legs. His fingers trailed slowly up her arm in a persuasive caress as he leaned forward and captured her mouth.

The pressure of his lips startled her and she stiffened, but all he did was lightly brush against her until she relaxed. It wasn't unpleasant, for his mouth was warm and tasted sweet from whatever beverage he'd been drinking when she'd arrived. His tongue traced the seam of her closed lips and then with gentle insistence, he forced it into her mouth.

She had never been kissed and didn't expect the rush of sensation. Heat, the sweep of his tongue, the firmness of his lips as they molded to hers…it all blended into an intimate sense of joining that had nothing remotely to do with the violation she anticipated.

The kiss lingered as he leisurely rubbed his tongue against hers, licked the sensitive corners of her lips, and even ran it along her teeth before sliding back deep inside again and again.

The entire time she could feel the hot throbbing of his erection against her stomach. It still felt huge, but Kartel was right. Her fears did seem to be abating. He hadn't forced himself on her in any way, she realized with relief, but was coaxing her with his light touch and gentle kisses.

"I like your taste," he whispered as he finally freed her mouth and slid a warm trail down the curve of her throat with his lips. "I will taste more in a moment. I'd bet you have a delicious pussy, and my tongue is anxious as hell to find out. But right now, your beautiful tits hold my attention. It's hard to believe these are real and not augmented."

He cupped one breast first, lifting and squeezing lightly and cradling the weight of it in his palm. His hands reshaped her resilient flesh and his thumb rubbed her nipple in a slow circle that teased the peak to sudden hardness. "Perfect." His voice was low and held satisfaction she could hear. "So full and firm and female."

She made an involuntary sound because the brush of the caress on that tingling crest sent a jolt through her stomach that centered between her legs. Delicious or not, her pussy suddenly felt warm and for whatever reason, wet.

Her reaction seemed to please him. "That's it," he murmured, his eyes darkened to shaded emerald as he toyed with her breast. "Let your body take over and free your mind, Jerra. Humans innately want sex and it was one characteristic we made sure to not eliminate as we evolved, so we do as well and even more so. Elevated to our level, your body will crave male possession. You may reject *why* this is happening between us, but I promise you won't reject *what* is happening."

She wanted to argue, but he began to fondle the other breast, and she lost her voice. Lying on her back, she watched him touch her. For a few minutes, she forgot about the window, but when she glanced over, she saw both of the other males were still there, watching as his mouth skimmed downward and settled over her erect nipple.

When he began to suckle, she had to fight to not move restlessly, not sure what exactly was happening. He moved back and forth, teasing one breast with the heated adhesion of his mouth, and then the other. She had no idea of his intentions when he suddenly rose above her, but the wet tip of his cock replaced his tongue. Semen glistened on her nipples as he pushed the head sensuously against her now stiff flesh, and she shivered in reaction.

"Spread your legs." The order was issued in a deeper tone and for a moment their gazes locked, his cock resting in the valley between her breasts, large and hot. She could feel the pulse against her much cooler flesh.

When she hesitated, he said with even conviction, "You are becoming aroused, Jerra. Don't you want to know what happens next? Spread your legs and I'll make you come." His arched brows lifted as he smiled darkly. "You won't be sorry to be introduced to that unique experience, believe me."

She did as she was told, mostly because he had been gentle so far, and she was a bit shocked at her own reaction to his touch. He was right. She had gone very quickly from resistant and angry, to expectant. Even the sight of his long cock rubbing against her nipples hadn't been nearly as shocking as it should have been. It normally would have gone against her instincts to open willingly, especially with a large naked and aroused male on top of her, but she spread her legs wide and felt the aching need between them with wonder.

Both Larik Armada and Colonel Helm would see what she was doing, she realized in her haze of confusion over the changes in her body and attitude. They witnessed her open-legged acquiescence and would expect the same thing.

There was a flash of approval in Ran Kartel's remarkable eyes and he slid downward slowly, leaving a wet trail of his seeping discharge on her torso. To her surprise, he didn't poise to enter her, but instead went all the way down until he rested in a prone position and his mouth settled on her exposed pussy.

What happened next was utterly shocking and incredible. The sensation of his warm tongue sliding between her labia, forcing the folds apart as he laved up and down, was not at all what she expected. He found a certain spot and teased it, swirling around the encased bundle of nerves with delectable pressure that made her wayward body arch in response. For the first time, she touched him, her hands grasping his broad shoulders. He felt solid and hot, and his skin was smooth and faintly damp.

She gasped. "Oh."

The pleasure was too exquisite to describe.

Almost mindless, she let her thighs fall apart even more, and he cupped her ass in his hands and accepted her offering. The soft wet sound of his mouth moving against her throbbing pussy was punctuated by her small involuntary moans filling the room. Through the haze of rapturous enjoyment, she felt an inner tension rise, as if her body sought something elusive.

A few moments later, she found it.

It was as if a star exploded in a blaze of glorious ecstasy, the brilliance of the release making her entire body shudder with the splendor of the pleasure. A low scream tore from her throat, and she could feel the contractions in her vagina and her womb as her orgasm held her prisoner.

It was beyond imaging and seemed to last forever until her body finally went limp and she felt him slide away.

Upwards. So he once again rested above her and this time she felt the nudge of something bold and hard against her wet, open pussy. Ran smiled, and his almost sinful beauty was striking and potent, reminding her of what and who he was. He drawled, "This is going to be a very pleasant journey, don't you think?"

* * * *

Her taste was still on his tongue and Ran let her savor her own sexual fluids as he kissed her and began penetration. The fact she was exquisitely tight was no surprise, for not only was her body innocent still, that was one of the perks of fucking human women. S-species males were larger than human males in every way, mentally and physically. His cock was bigger than what her body was designed to accept, but what was remarkable about human female anatomy, and especially the vagina, was the elasticity of that organ. It always took a little time to get all the way in, and it was pleasurable as hell, but he knew she could take all of him if he was careful. Compared to sex with one of his own kind, her tightness made the experience all the more enjoyable. Luckily, in her case, she was still almost dazed from her first orgasmic experience, and as he slowly worked his cock through her small opening and began to push into the wet heat of her hot, sweet pussy, she didn't seem to register the discomfort at his entry.

If there *were* any discomfort, he realized in some small astonishment as he gave her another inch so slowly, he broke out in a sweat. All he sensed coming from the woman below him was pleasure and her mind had been sending him signals like a beacon the entire time.

Sure enough, a moment later, she made a small sound like a sigh, and her lashes fluttered open as she slightly lifted her pelvis in an instinctive and unspoken invitation.

Yes, she definitely—or her body—wanted him inside her.

Her inner walls were like heaven around the careful invasion, yielding just enough to allow him in, hugging him like a clenched fist. Usually, he had complete control sexually, but whether it was the abstinence of the past few weeks as they readied for the journey and made the trip past Earth to pick up their females, or the way her delicious pussy felt around his cock, he already had the urge to ejaculate. Ran took a deep shuddering breath and fought it, sinking in deeper until he finally reached his goal and his entire length was sheathed in her luscious body.

Jerra moaned and he asked through clenched teeth, "Am I hurting you?"

"I feel torn in half." She breathed the words in small pants. "But there isn't pain."

"You feel damned good," he told her with complete honesty, marveling at not only the pleasure of her pussy holding him deep inside her, but her remarkable and entirely natural beauty. She lay beneath him, framed in the glory of her lustrous outspread golden hair, her beautiful body tinted a lovely post-orgasmic pink. Those full high breasts quivered as she breathed, tipped with delicate rose nipples that had tasted as sweet as any confection.

The amazing fact was her alluring perfection wasn't engineered or manipulated by science—but the simple result of random genetics. He was sure he had never seen a woman so lovely even among S-species females, all of whom were gorgeous. "Tell me when you have adjusted enough to my size that I can move. I know I'm big, and sometimes it takes a few moments."

Her smooth brow knitted. "Move?"

By law, human females were kept as ignorant of sex as possible until a certain age, just so they could be taken for pleasure and breeding purposes if S-species chose them. He wasn't surprised she didn't entirely understand what happened during intercourse. "In and out," he explained hoarsely, wondering if he would explode at once the minute he started. "The friction will make me climax sexually, and you too, if done the right way."

She bit her soft lower lip and just slightly raised her hips. "I see."

"Do you? I'll be happy to demonstrate." He wasn't sure he could wait any longer anyway, so he slid backwards and was rewarded by a small gasp. With his size, the hardness of his cock rubbed against her clitoris and he felt the small shudder of her reaction to the sensuous gliding pressure.

He thrust back in slowly, still aware of her vulnerable smallness. She felt almost delicate in his arms. Yet when she arched her neck back and tilted her pelvis up to take his entire length, the motion was inherently sexual. Even though she hadn't been bred to pleasure men, she also seemed to naturally have that trait as well, because while the added hormones were a boost, she had still climaxed very swiftly.

He wasn't sure he'd ever been so aroused and a small bead of sweat rolled down his jaw. Ran began to move a little faster, backwards swiftly, and forward with deliberate care, nudging her cervix with his engorged tip so he felt softness give to his size. Her hands grasped his shoulders with increasing urgency, as if she needed to hold onto something, and she matched his rhythm with amazing instinctive movements of her hips.

Definitely a natural.

The control he prided himself on stretched, slipped, and finally snapped when she suddenly tightened her thighs around his surging hips and her inner muscles clenched. Jerra's nails dug into his rigid muscles as his own orgasm roared through his body and he felt the pain with a sense of elation because simultaneous climax was rare enough and this was…miraculous.

He was sure he had never come with such force and pleasure in his life. His cock flexed as he poured a torrent of sperm deep in her contracting pussy and the white-hot rapture made his mind go blank for a few long, exquisite moments. When he finally caught his breath, he rolled to his side, his muscles quivering and weak, and pulled her with him. He kept his cock buried inside her on purpose, because it felt damned good still and the fit was so uniquely snug, as if her body was reluctant to let him withdraw.

The post-coital silence was peaceful, and she didn't seem to want to break it either. Sprawled across his chest, her legs still open to his carnal possession, she lay quiet and acquiescent in his embrace. He let his fingers drift through her soft hair as his racing heart finally slowed to a more normal pace. Patiently, he waited, for he could feel her confusion.

After a while, she lifted her head from where it rested on his chest and looked at him directly. "Will the others be like you?"

The question was no surprise. He smiled, enchanted with the challenge in her azure eyes. "I have never had sex with either one of them, so how do I know?" Then he dropped the light-hearted tone, knowing his honest answer would ease her restless fears. "I was just teasing. If you're asking if they will they take care to make sure you enjoy it, they will. Both the colonel and Larik

Armada are fine men. We all agreed you should be made to want to please us sexually rather than dread it." He stroked her cheek with a forefinger. "I take it from the marks on my back, you'd agree to do it again with me."

"It is rather hard to answer that question when you are still inside me," she answered tartly. With her halo of shimmering hair and pale, silken skin, she looked like a goddess in the old human legends, too flawless to be true.

"I like being inside you." Ran could hear the huskiness in his voice. "I'm asking for a purpose, also. I'll be hard again soon. It's happening already."

Her eyes widened. "You want to do it again, right now?"

"Yes." Before she could answer, he cupped her nape and pulled her down for a long, heated kiss. With amazing swiftness, he could feel the lengthening of his returning erection. He rocked his hips up so he rubbed against her clit and she moaned into his mouth, her sensitized body responding.

As far as he was concerned, it was his answer.

* * * *

Ian shifted in his chair uncomfortably, his brooding gaze fastened on the room through the window. Idly, he lifted his glass to his mouth. The level of liquid in the bottle at his elbow had diminished to almost nothing and Larik had hardly had much before he excused himself and went to his private quarters.

It wasn't good to overindulge, and Ian rarely did, but lately, he was uncharacteristically restless.

Damn Captain Kia Liale for that.

Shit, he really, really wanted her, and the couple on the bed did not help matters in any way. Now he had a rock hard erection and nothing to do with it.

Narrowing his eyes, he tried to ignore the uncomfortable bulge in his pants and watched.

There was no question the human captive was beautiful. They had all been stunned by her lovely face and incredible body, especially since it was entirely natural. Silky blond hair, pale blue eyes, and a soft sultry pink mouth…yes, he was attracted to her. Who wouldn't be? Besides, she had gorgeous breasts for someone so slender. Her rose-colored nipples were small and dainty, and her skin much more pale than any S-species woman, since the diverse races from Earth had long ago been integrated into their genetic make up. Ian admired breasts in all shapes and sizes, and the woman now making love with Kartel for the second time certainly had a spectacular set.

She must be satisfying in bed, also, for Kartel had barely finished the first time and was at it again.

Ian saw his friend lean forward and whisper something in the woman's ear, his mouth nuzzling her neck as his hips began to move. His cock was still buried deep between her spread thighs, and his buttocks flexed as he pulled out partially and sank back in. Her breasts moved with each thrust, the opulent flesh shifting erotically.

It was actually very arousing to watch both Kartel's obvious enjoyment, and her evident pleasure in the way he fucked her. Whatever fears she night have had, Ran had done his usual smoothing of the troubled waters and she was now taking him easily, her slim legs bent at the knee and spread wide open so his long body fit between them.

She was very small. Ian saw how carefully Ran had entered her, and with his own huge size, he would have to be especially cautious.

With Kia, there was no need for such restraint, he mused in wayward memory. She matched him, wild need for wild need. Their one encounter had been foolish, for it was against the rules to fraternize sexually with another officer, but he could still remember the tempestuous physical joy of it. Nothing about it resembled lovemaking. They had fucked each other, pure and simple. Her wet cunt and his eager cock coming together in a fierce and exultant experience that made him wonder if he would ever forget it and move on.

Because he really had no choice but to put it behind him. It was a hard and fast rule, and punishable in ways that would ruin his military career if they were ever caught again together. He simply should not sleep with anyone in his command because it was political suicide to do so.

No matter what he wanted.

So, he would have to make do with their alluring captive and forget his impractical infatuation.

Morosely, he reached for the bottle to drain it.

Chapter 3

Jerra opened her eyes slowly and felt disoriented when she gazed at the ceiling. It had been painted to simulate the vastness of space, with tiny stars against a dark background, but was static.

No, she wasn't in the cubicle any longer.

Cautiously, she raised her head and looked around. All she saw were pale walls, no furniture but the bed where she lay amidst the tumbled sheets, and the one window into the center room.

Oh, God. She fell back and shut her eyes again. Her body felt odd, a little sticky and well used, and there was a slight soreness between her legs. It all came flooding back and she rested against the softness of the mattress as she remembered every detail.

Ran Kartel had been both gentle and wickedly demanding, and in the end, he had taken her sexually three times before she drifted off into an exhausted sleep. The man had been huge, she recalled with a flush invading her cheeks, but somehow, her body had been able to adjust to that impressive size, and it had felt…well, if she were honest about it, wonderful.

She had liked it.

All of it. The way he kissed her—as if her taste and essence were something he craved—the scent of his skin, the impressive hardness of his very male body. He'd used his mouth on her pussy, and though she'd been shocked, it had felt sublime. The actual consummation hadn't been what she expected, either, not at all degrading but the opposite, as if something profound had happened between them. She did not feel like an unwilling slave, but a woman who had shared an exquisite experience with a male who had also enjoyed it.

A treacherous curl of excitement shot through her stomach. If the evening before had been an indication of the next months of confinement, it would not be anything like what she imagined.

The need to relieve herself made her finally crawl out of bed. Outside the window, the common room was empty, for which she was grateful. It still made her uncomfortable the men could see her almost all the time, but they were either in their own sleeping quarters or gone. Nude, she padded to the cleansing room and used the facilities. There was a small square glass enclosure and she figured out the mechanism with only a small amount of difficulty and gratefully stepped into the stream of warm water. It soothed away the tenderness in her breasts and she washed the dried residue from her body, seeing the streaks on her thighs with wonder at the prodigious amount. S-species probably produced more sperm than ordinary humans at a guess, for everything else about them was enhanced and superior.

Despite the gush of the warm water, she shivered slightly. The engineer they called Armada was as tall as Ran Kartel and had the same lean build. But the other one, Colonel Helm, was enormous. The thought of him taking her was daunting.

But also exciting.

It was shameful, but her pussy suddenly felt hot and wet as she imagined it. The heat and rush of moisture embarrassed her, and Jerra wondered at her purely physical reaction. Undoubtedly, it was the injection, plus the ambassador had done a very good job of her initiation into the pleasures of sexual intercourse. Never in her life had she imagined such acute sensation possible. How he held her afterwards was a revelation also, for she didn't realize how frightened she'd been the past days since she'd been captured. The way his strong arms had cradled her against his powerful body made her feel safe and protected. Though, when she thought about it, they had just met and it was an illusion, albeit a pleasant one.

Well, more than just met, considering what they'd done together. She blushed again, grateful no one could see it.

After washing her hair, she carefully dried it and found in a small cabinet a comb and other necessities. Refreshed, she stepped outside with a towel wrapped around her body, and realized with a small grimace her only article of clothing still consisted of the pale blue, barely-there gown. She slipped it on, ran the comb through her long curls one more time, and went out into the center room.

It was a relief to see a covered tray sat on the table. When she lifted the lid, she found the typical type of food she had been fed so far on the ship. The substances on the plate didn't look familiar but tasted actually quite good. The strip of something that tasted like beef helped ease her hunger, and other similarly shaped items represented vegetables or fruits. The beverage left for her also had a strange but not unpleasant taste, and as hungry as she was, she didn't turn up her nose. She ate almost everything, and replaced the lid.

Now what should she do?

Fed, clean, and apparently all alone, she went curiously to the door that accessed the ship. It was activated by a device that scanned the eye of the individual who wanted to open it, and she tried, only to see a flashing red light that made her step back immediately and blink. It wasn't a huge surprise she was a prisoner and confined to the cabin space, but it still made the panicked feeling return a little.

What did they expect her to do when they weren't using her for the purpose she had been kidnapped to fulfill? She was not just a body, but also had a mind, and she was used to being active. She had worked back on Earth as a surgical nurse in a prestigious hospital. She had to wonder if the S-species bothered to explain the disappearance when they took someone. Surely her parents would inform the facility what had happened to her, and since females were appropriated often enough, no one would be surprised. Every female human was aware of the possibility. She just hadn't expected it to happen to her.

The hiss of the pressurized mechanism that trigged the door made her feel a nervous thrill. It wasn't Ran Kartel but instead the young engineer, Armada. She took another instinctive step back as he came through the doorway and eyed him warily. His fair good looks were striking, and up close, he was quite young, probably not more than a few years older than herself. He wore the typical tunic, fitted trousers, and polished boots, and they suited his almost slim, tall build. Lieutenant Herad had called him brilliant, and surely it must be true if he were the designer of the engine that propelled the giant ship so efficiently from galaxy to galaxy.

"Hello." He smiled at her and his gaze skimmed her nearly bare body briefly before politely lifting to her face. "Did you see the food?"

"Yes, thank you."

"Kartel tells me your given name is Jerra."

"Yes."

"I hope you don't mind if I use it." His smile was open and boyishly appealing, nothing like the wickedly attractive curve of Ran Kartel's mouth. "You must also call me Larik. We are going to be good friends, after all."

"That's an interesting way of putting it." Jerra couldn't help the sarcasm. Yes, the night before had been like a sinful, pleasurable dream, but she was still a prisoner.

He caught the inflection in her voice because his brows went up a fraction, but he didn't comment. Instead, he went over to the wall and pressed a small button she hadn't even noticed. A panel slid open and revealed a galley, and more importantly, an entire section of screens. "You were asleep when I left or I would have explained to you that there are methods for your entertainment in your leisure time. Food, also, if you get hungry between the times when our meals are delivered. Would you like me to show you how it all works? You can read, or watch films from varied planets, including your own. Games are also available to play at the touch of your hand. There is no need for you to be bored."

Well, that was something, for she thought it was less than humane to leave her trapped in a small space with nothing to do. "Yes, please show me," she said, not trying to conceal her eagerness. "I was just wondering what to do with myself."

He glanced over and his vivid cobalt eyes lit with laughter. "You needn't ever worry about what to do with yourself, Jerra. We'll do plenty enough with you to take care of that. But if you want a distraction now and then, I will explain."

As heat rushed into her face, she wonder if she would blush all the way to wherever they were headed. "I would appreciate it."

He was definitely an engineer for as he began to explain how to work the various screens, from book readers to projection, he also added so many details about how the machines themselves worked that finally, laughing, she had to stop him. "Just tell me what buttons to push," Jerra pleaded. "My mind is beginning to spin."

"Oh." He looked disconcerted, and then shook his head ruefully. "I apologize. I tend to get carried away. Machines speak to me. I love them and I forget not everyone feels the same sometimes. Let me try to just go over the basics."

"I think that would be better."

She stood close enough to him as he took a simpler approach and began again, she could smell the spicy scent of his cologne. It was masculine and intriguing. Against her will, she found herself watching him from under the veil of her lashes.

In turn, she saw his gaze stray more than once over the thin material that did little to conceal her breasts. He glanced down lower too, to where her bare legs were exposed by the shortness of her skirt.

When he finished the explanations, he moved casually to a small shelf and selected a bottle of greenish liquid. "Would you like a glass of wine?"

"My father doesn't allow alcohol, so I've never had wine."

Armada raised his brows. "Your father no longer dictates your actions, Jerra."

It was so bizarre to have been at home less than a week before, living her sedate, sheltered life, and now she was on a ship speeding toward another world, living with three men who were complete strangers. She was no longer on Earth. Apparently her parents had reconciled themselves to her fate, and according to Lieutenant Herad, had even been paid for her. She didn't precisely blame them, for there was no choice if the S-species selected a young woman, so it seemed ludicrous to still abide by their rules any longer. "You're right and I think I would, yes."

He poured two glasses and motioned for her to sit at the table. "We can drink this and talk awhile."

She accepted the invitation, though she lifted one brow skeptically. "You wish to talk?"

"For now." He sank down in an opposite chair. "We have plenty of time. All afternoon, in fact. Neither one of the others will be back until late. They have meetings today to discuss strategies when we arrive at Septinium."

"Why are we going there?" She wasn't sure she could ask in her position, but it didn't hurt to try.

Luckily, he didn't seem to mind. He sat back in his chair, his long legs extended comfortably, and frowned. "The people there are war-like and a bit primitive. They are raiding nearby planets and causing tension everywhere. Our government wants to avoid an interstellar war. Yes, we can step in if it happens and intercede, but prevention saves lives. Kartel is an expert with this sort of thing, though even he seems doubtful this time. However, he, like

Colonel Helm, goes where he is told. Diplomacy first, but military action if necessary. That's why they are both here."

"I see." She sipped her wine and found it actually a bit sweet, the taste lingering on her tongue. "And why are you here? I know you invented the engine, but isn't the ship running smoothly?"

"Her maiden voyage. I am along to make *sure* she stays running smoothly and to help the technicians understand her."

"Her? You sound as if it is alive."

A glimmering smile curved his mouth. "To me, she is. I created her and gave her life."

"That's an interesting take on it, I suppose."

"What of you, Jerra? Will you be able to acclimate to your new life?" His handsome face bore true curiosity and what seemed like genuine concern.

"Do I have a choice?"

"You seemed to enjoy last night."

The word 'embarrassment' took on a whole new meaning at that blunt observation. She couldn't help but glance at the window and remember he had watched her sexual abandon and seen her entirely naked. "It wasn't what I expected," she managed to say in a strangled voice.

"There's more. And with each of us it will be different, I imagine. Sex is a varied world and pleasure comes in all forms." The timbre of his voice dropped just a telltale notch. "When we finish our wine, I will show you. You'll like it, I promise."

She looked at him helplessly, her fingers tightening on the stem of her glass. Then, because she was truly curious, she asked, "I don't understand the window. If it is to demean your prisoners, it isn't necessary. I understand full well I have to cooperate."

His fine brows drew together. "You think it's to demean you?"

"Why else would you allow me no privacy?"

He gave her a direct look from those startlingly blue eyes. "It's there because we like to look at you, of course. It also serves to let us know if you are busy or sleeping, and besides, I'm afraid males are very visual creatures. In short, we like to watch. I may have not been the one between your legs last night, but I enjoyed it just the same. I had to go to my quarters and relieve myself manually."

The explanation was made without any apology or embarrassment and Jerra wondered if she would ever attain such a pragmatic attitude toward the act of sex. She supposed she might, given her circumstances, and in fact, probably should do her best to achieve it as soon as possible. "I suppose I don't really know much about men," she admitted.

"S-species are not ordinary males like on your planet, either, but you'll learn. Actually, there is little for you to worry about, Jerra. All you have to do is be willing to give us what we want and if I am a judge from your response to Kartel, it won't be a chore for you. He claims there is something very unique about you beyond your beautiful face and desirable body, and I am anxious as hell to find out what exactly he means. Tell me, are you finished with your wine?"

She had finished, and felt a little light-headed since she had expected to be dragged straight to her bed. Instead he had sat and conversed with her like she was a guest—not a slave held for his pleasure—so she found it much easier to nod and stand. He motioned for her to precede him into the room, and she did, surprised to feel very little apprehension.

Turning to face him, she said with resignation, "I suppose you want me to take off my gown."

"Let me." He stepped closer and caught the hem, skimming his fingers up the outside of her thighs and hips as he eased the material upward and over her head. He tossed it carelessly aside and stared down at her bared breasts with undisguised longing. "You have no idea how much I want to fuck you."

She had some idea, for the impressive bulge in his fitted dark pants was a pretty obvious indication. When he took her in his arms and bent his head to lower his mouth to hers, she could feel the rigid hardness of his erection through the material, pressed against the softness of her stomach. A jolt of excitement shot through her and his mouth was warm and insistent as he kissed her. The experience was completely different than when Ran had done the same thing, but still very enjoyable. His hands cupped her bare ass and pulled her tighter against his hard body and aroused cock and he gave a low groan into her mouth.

"Get in bed," he ordered. "I'll be right back."

As she climbed on the bed, she saw him disappear into her small cleansing room and emerge a moment later with something in his hand. It looked like a small oblong capsule about the length of her little finger but narrower. She had actually noticed a box of them in the cabinet that held the other necessities provided for her and wondered what they were.

"Lie back." He gently pushed her to a supine position and lifted her knees so they were bent and her feet rested on the mattress. "Open for me."

Jerra eyed the item in his hand uncertainly and kept her thighs clamped together. "What is that?"

"Relax." He pushed her legs apart so her pussy was exposed and open and his gaze glittered like brilliant sapphires as he stared at it. "The doctor has provided these for all the human females taken and brought on board. When inserted, it will melt quickly and act not only as a lubricant to ease any soreness from last night, but enhances your pleasure. With three of us regularly sharing your bed, you will want to use these on a daily basis, I suspect."

Since she was a little sore, the idea was probably a good one and it was heartening to have further proof her captors cared at all about the comfort of their prisoners. When he parted her labia, found her vaginal entrance, and inserted the capsule, she didn't protest. With one long finger he pushed it in as far as possible and she actually suppressed a sigh of pleasure at the intimate invasion.

Almost immediately she felt the warmth of the dissolving lubricant and a strange sense of loss when Larik slid his finger free.

"It should feel good, I'm told." He began to undress, his gaze still fastened on the apex of her open legs. His tunic was tossed aside without care to expose a muscular chest, his boots jerked off as quickly as possible, and when he unfastened his pants and pushed them down his hips, his swollen erection jutted forward. He wasn't as wide-shouldered as Ran Kartel, but just as athletically built, without an ounce of fat on his body. She had no idea if his cock was as big, but it certainly looked intimidating and large and she took in a shuddering breath as she remembered how it felt to be stretched so impossibly wide.

"It does feel good." Whether it was the wine, the injection, the aphrodisiac in the capsule, or something that had nothing to do with any of them, she didn't modestly close her legs, but stayed the way he positioned her, knees bent and thighs open. She could feel the soft mattress at her back, the smoothness of the sheets, and most acutely the tingling in her pussy and breasts.

She wanted him inside her, she realized with a small shock.

He took her position for the invitation it was and knelt between her parted thighs. Very lightly he rubbed the head of his stiff penis over her clitoris and she felt a streak of blissful pleasure. He continued to stimulate her with his cock in one hand, the swollen, weeping tip pressing against the most sensitive spot on her body until she openly moaned.

"By the stars, Jerra, you are so beautiful," he told her in an echo of Ran's compliment of the night before. He leaned forward and licked one upright nipple, still teasing her clit with his cock. "I want to see you come," he whispered against her breast.

Her hands slid into the silk of his blond hair and she closed her eyes, letting sensation take over. "Oh…oh."

When he sucked the aching crest into the heated recess of his mouth, she felt her stomach muscles contract in response. Still kneeling, he used his free hand to massage one breast, suckled the other, and continued the erotic friction of hard flesh against her swelling clit.

It felt too good, too wicked, and so all-consuming all conscious thought centered between her legs and his teasing cock.

The rush of her climax took her by surprise. Suddenly, she arched and cried out, the first rapturous spasm so acute it made her shake wildly. The pulsing between her legs was accompanied by her womb contracting and a rush of moisture into her pussy as he kept his slick crest against her clit for what seemed like an eternity.

Then he moved, the pressure refocused lower, and Jerra felt him shift, his arms braced to keep his weight balanced.

"Open your legs wider to help me." Larik's face was intent, and his beautiful eyes half-closed. "Human females are so damned tight and it always takes some work to get inside."

She obeyed, spreading as far as possible, wondering as she had the night before if he could actually fit. The engorged head distended the opening of her pussy and pressed forward and she felt her inner muscles resist the unnatural widening but give as he slowly entered her with inexorable carnal demand.

Arms locked on either side of her shoulders, he loomed above her and the fierce expression on his face told her he was experiencing the same almost painful pleasure of invasion and acceptance. The lubricant must have helped for this penetration was much easier, and in half the time, his long cock was sunk to the hilt.

"This first time will be fast. Sorry, but I've been without a female for weeks." His voice was low and hoarse. "But I can be ready again very quickly, don't worry."

She wasn't worried...she was frantic for him to move. When he began to withdraw, she felt the fluid drag of his rigid flesh with heightened sensitivity and ran her hands along his tight buttocks in a plea for more. He obliged, sinking back inside fully, impaling her so full, she felt completely possessed. Very quickly his thrusts became harder and less controlled and they were both gasping and trembling in sync.

"I'm coming," Larik gritted out, his bare chest brushing her erect nipples as he thrust deeply and stopped moving. Incredibly, she could feel the immense rush of his release as hot liquid filled her with a forceful flood. As his cock swelled to release his seed, the subtly increased pressure on her clit was all she needed. Jerra screamed and her fingers dug into the small of his back as she convulsed around him.

"Oh shit." He jerked in response, his cock flexing.

The universe flattened and went away in a dazzling rush. All she could feel was the rapturous pulse of her inner contractions and the flex of his sex as she milked his seed from him. Gradually, they both began to relax.

With his weight braced enough to keep from crushing her, he lay solidly on top of her and she felt very small in comparison. She could smell the clean tang of his sweat, both foreign and now familiar. When she regained her breath, she tentatively ran her fingers up the length of his spine. He quivered at the caress, his face still buried in her tumbled hair.

Larik lifted his head and grinned then, a purely male curve of his mouth that indicated his satisfaction. He stroked her bare hip. "Kartel didn't lie. You're an amazing female, Jerra. I was not looking forward to this long, dull journey, but I have changed my mind."

Chapter 4

Ran looked around the council room and deliberately gauged the expression on the face of each individual. The opinion was certainly divided and he had the grim feeling that whatever happened when they arrived at Septinium, he would be the one to make the final decision. He said with neutral inflection, "I realize the Minoa government is well-represented here, but we brought along military support for a reason. If Colonel Helm is getting information indicating a strong show of strength when we reach the planet is best, I trust his judgment."

Ian looked impassive at the comment. "I'm getting more and more information each day, but we are still far away. Maybe the situation will change, but if it doesn't, we cannot send in a diplomatic team without protection."

"You'll cause a fight," one of the Council protested vehemently. "The Septinium forces will react predictably to soldiers arriving in their world."

"Maybe." Ran was getting tired of the debate since they were still months away. "We'll have to weigh the facts as they come in, and judge the best course then. In the meantime, we are adjourned for today."

He rose and so did everyone else, and naturally Ian fell into step beside him as they headed back toward their quarters. Ian muttered, "Damn politicians. They want to make the rest of civilization think we are not despotic tyrants. I say the only way to rule something as vast as what we control is to let rogue worlds know they can't step over the line."

"I agree," Ran said wearily. "I know firsthand diplomacy does not always work. Sometimes, it backfires with disastrous results. But I am told to try."

"And I am told to not let you die doing it." Ian looked formidably stubborn as they strode through the long corridor.

"I appreciate the sentiment, believe me." Ran gave his friend a wry smile. They had known each other for a long time, and the friendship had sprung first from mutual respect, blossomed into recognition of similar strengths and goals, and then genuine affection.

In minutes, they reached their destination and Ran wanted desperately to have a drink and relax for a few minutes. Actually, he wouldn't have minded a bit to relax in an entirely pleasurable different way, but quite simply, it wasn't his turn. The evening before, they returned to find Armada and the lovely naked Jerra entwined and asleep, and Helm had been patient, but it was definitely his night.

Ran gave a sidelong glance at his dark-haired companion as they reached the right level and scanned in. "You've never taken a human female?"

"No." Ian admitted. "They are so small. Trust me, most of them take one look at me and want to faint. S-species females are much easier."

"Like Captain Liale?"

Ian's face darkened. "It was once, and a bad idea. I had too much to drink. We both knew better and could be disciplined for the slip. How the hell do you even know it happened?"

"Just being in the room with the two of you tells me something happened. Please, Ian, I am who I am."

"And damned uncomfortable it can be for your friends, Ran."

"All right, we won't talk about the pretty captain but Jerra instead. The experience is like none other, believe me, when you are inside her."

Ian gave him a sardonic look. "So it seemed the other night. You certainly enjoyed yourself."

"I did," Ran agreed, remembering silken thighs and her almost painful—but entirely pleasurable—tight heat. "Our gorgeous captive is so responsive, I think you will agree it elevates sex to a different level."

"Sex is sex," Ian argued. "One orgasm isn't different from another."

"I'll be curious to know if you say the same thing after sampling Jerra's incredible body. There's something about fucking a female that really likes it."

"You're certain she can take me?"

"Think of it this way, Ian. The vagina on a human female can allow a fully formed fetus to go through it, so while you may be big, you aren't that big. She'll be tight, yes, so tight you'll want to shoot your load as you even try to get in, but the effort is worth it. Once you're there and you hear those soft sounds she makes as she comes…I am telling you, it's going to be unique."

"That's what Armada claims." The colonel ducked his imposing height through the doorway. "I'm getting more intrigued all the time by our beautiful human."

Only she isn't who you really want, Ran thought with unerring conviction.

* * * *

She had gulped down two glasses of wine with dinner, but she wasn't sure it was enough. Jerra was pleased they wished to include her when they ate their meals, however sitting at the table with three such tall, imposing men was a little uncomfortable, though they treated her respectfully and with solicitude. Tonight she knew what was going to happen afterwards, and it was confirmed by the speculative looks Ian Helm sent at her across the table. The tall colonel was a contrast to the clean-cut good looks of the other two men, having an almost satanic male beauty that matched his incredible physique. Rather like everything else that was rationed out on the ship, she was sure it was due for the brawny soldier to have his time with her.

It was frightening, but then again, her experiences so far had been wonderful and though his sheer size made her nervous, there was an element of exhilaration over the idea of him taking her sexually that made her pulse race.

The dishes were taken away, and her empty glass, and she still sat there, not sure what was expected.

When he stood, she felt her mouth go dry for he was so tall, she barely came up to the middle of his chest. He looked pointedly at her bedroom, and then her face, asking in a matter-of-fact tone, "Are you ready?"

The direct approach was probably not surprising from a military man who commanded men and directed battles, but it left her momentarily at a loss for words. She was also acutely aware of Larik and Ran, lounging in their chairs, obviously ready to watch everything.

No, she wasn't going to think about that.

She swallowed and nodded, rising on wobbly legs. He followed her in, shut the door, and looked at her with eyes so dark, they were as ebony as his glossy long hair. He said coolly, "I am not a smooth diplomat like Kartel, nor a brainy intellectual like Armada. However, I would never hurt a female, quite the opposite, so don't look at me as if I was going to eat you alive. Prisoner or not, you can rest assured if anything happens to threaten the expedition, I would die to protect you."

That speech—made without inflection but obviously sincere—made her blink. Not sure what to say, Jerra stood with her arms at her side and tilted her head up to stare into his face, seeing the elegant planes and angles in a new light, and noting his dark eyes held a soft light at odds with his formidable presence. She stammered, "I...I appreciate that, for I was sure I was not significant, except in the most base of ways."

He lifted one ebony brow in an arch and a surprisingly warm smile lit his face. "On the contrary, you seem to have had a powerful impact on our companions. I'm assured this will be an experience to remember."

He meant sexually, of course, but still, the idea anyone cared enough about her to offer protection was moving. She slipped her dress off and tossed it aside. Nude, knowing the other two watched through the window, she gave him a return smile. They'd both seen it before, so why should she be embarrassed? "Is that a challenge, Colonel?"

Heat flared in his eyes as his gaze raked her nude body. "Maybe."

"I accept." She turned and walked with deliberate nonchalance toward the cleansing room. Once inside, she opened the cupboard and took out one of the capsules, shut the door, and then changed her mind and took out another of the lubricants. She inserted them, though she had never touched herself so intimately much less pushed her finger inside her pussy. She was warm and soft inside, and hopefully, very elastic.

The telltale warmth of the dissolving tablets made her breasts instantly tight and her nipples taut. She walked back out to find Colonel Helm almost completely undressed. He tossed his last boot aside and unfastened his pants.

Good God.

She had expected him to be very big. Huge, even, for Ran and Larik were big enough she had been apprehensive about their possession. But this time she was...stunned.

His massive erection was so long and thick, she stopped walking and stared, all her bravado banished. It was obvious he was S-species. No human could ever have such a large penis, though she was not an expert on the subject.

"Don't be afraid." The reassurance was made in a quiet voice that belied the fierceness of his arousal. "We can do this so you are in control, Jerra. Just come here."

In control of...*that*?

When she didn't move, he took the initiative and lay down on the bed on his back. He didn't look any less enormous in that position, but at least he wasn't looming over her. She took a quivering step and another, not sure if she was fascinated or simply hypnotized by his erection.

"You can be on top," he said softly, watching her cautious approach. "Take it as you wish, as far as you can. I won't even touch you if you don't want me to."

She had pleased the others, and he was being just as courteous and considerate, and she wanted to do the same for him. Not because of some duty she'd been told she owed by her captors, but because they treated her well and made her feel desired, not simply used. "Tell me what to do."

"Did you use a capsule?" His dark hair was a stark contrast to the white sheets.

A choked laugh gurgled from her throat and her gaze remained fixed on his cock. "Two."

"Good idea." He chuckled, the sound reassuring. "As much as you worry I am too large, I am concerned you are too small."

"Maybe we shouldn't try."

"Maybe we should." He lay there, dwarfing the bed, his nude body truly magnificent. "I need you and as Ran pointed out to me, your body is designed to accommodate more than just this." He ran his finger along his swollen length as she watched and semen oozed from the large slit in the head.

Jerra could feel the effects of the two capsules and her pussy seemed to soften and weep with need. She was afraid of his enormous size, yet somehow wanted it, too. Squaring her shoulders, she climbed onto the bed. Effortlessly, he spanned her hips with his large hands and lifted her so she straddled him. His large erection lay high on his stomach, and she stared at it.

His hands, long-fingered and graceful for one whose art was war, slid upward and cupped her breasts. She sank her teeth into her lower lip to fight a moan and involuntarily arched backwards, thrusting her nipples against his palms. In turn, he fondled her and watched her reaction through heavy-lidded eyes. He resembled a warrior prince, with a web work of silvery scars across the heavily muscled plane of his chest, and his thick dark hair. "Such spectacular tits," he murmured, rubbing her nipples with his fingers. The pressure was hard enough to make her take in a swift breath, yet also seductively gentle. "You see," he pointed out in that same quiet and steady voice as he stroked her pliant flesh to erect points, "you do want to try. You're soaking wet, Jerra. Take me in your hand."

She looked at him at first in confusion, but when he lifted her easily, she understood.

Wrapping her fingers around his girth, she positioned the flared crest at her entrance and felt her pussy stretch wide open as he slowly began to lower her onto his cock. Bracing her hands on his chest, she squirmed to try to force him in and for a moment she thought it was as impossible as it looked, but slowly, with his hands supporting her weight, she absorbed the tip.

"Oh, God," she moaned and sank a little lower, not sure if it was pleasure or pain, or a beguiling combination of both. He was hot and hard and so big she could not get her fingers entirely around him.

"Yes." The word was a low hiss and his eyes closed briefly. "Oh, fuck, that's good. More."

"I'm trying." Panting, almost wild with need now, she let her weight and the lubricant help her as she took more of his cock into her now burning pussy. The sheer size of it made her want to scream with pleasure for her labia was pulled apart and her clit was hard against his satiny, rock-hard length.

It felt impossibly good and she rocked, sucking in a breath at the discomfort coupled with ecstasy as she slid downward, taking more, more than she thought possible, until she realized incredulously he was in completely and her buttocks rested on the cradle of his hips.

Ian caressed her inner thighs with his thumbs, still holding her hips. "I can wait until you are adjusted to move. There's no hurry."

"Yes, there is," she told him, staring into his dark eyes, knowing her entire body was flushed with need. She could feel the heat in her cheeks, her breasts, and especially in her aching, stretched pussy. "Lift me a little," she pleaded. "I'm so close."

"I never disappoint a lady," he muttered, her weight seemingly incidental as he eased her up and let her slowly back down.

That easily, she started to come. The first ripple tightened her already overfilled passage around his cock and she went wild, grasping his bulging biceps and unable to keep the orgasm at bay any longer. Head back, her long hair streaming down her back, she clenched around him and her inner muscles shook with the strain of his penetration.

It was incredible, and she gasped out a weak cry before she slid forward against him.

"I've got you," he whispered in her ear. "I need to finish."

He rolled, and she let him take her until she was on her back. He slid out a little bit the first time and gently pushed back in against her softened, slick flesh, and when she showed no sign of discomfort, began a more assertive rhythm of thrusts in and out. Beneath his large body, she felt overwhelmed, and not just by his size, but by what was happening to her. The pain was gone or incidental and all she felt was his carnal cadence and the joining of their bodies.

She climaxed again almost immediately in complete joyous abandon, and he suddenly gave a fierce growl and pulled back a fraction so when he erupted inside her, the forceful hot gush didn't cause pain. His testicles were the size of her bunched fists and she felt what seemed to be an endless stream of sperm pump against the mouth of her womb.

Afterwards, when he eased free, she felt hollow inside, as if something were missing. He cradled her close and it felt a little like being held by a rock, except for his long, passionate kisses and the reverent way he explored her body with his hands.

Three gorgeous, considerate lovers and months to enjoy them, she thought sleepily as he nuzzled her neck.

Perhaps being captured wasn't so bad after all.

* * * *

Ran sipped his wine and stared through the window at the sleeping girl. The artificial light spilled over her golden hair and lent it highlights of pale platinum. She lay on her side like a child, one hand beneath her cheek, and with the sheet to her waist, her bare, ivory breasts quivered a little with each deep breath. Long lashes lay like delicate shadows on her cheeks.

It was odd, but he had never felt jealousy before. Well, maybe it still wasn't jealousy, maybe it was something else, but he could not think what. Yes, he'd watched her with Ian, seen her enjoyment, and being what and who he was, knew she'd felt afraid at first, but had courageously overcome it and found pleasure instead.

She was remarkable. Incredible. Special in a way that wasn't just sexual. He sensed their intertwined destinies even before the lieutenant had ushered her into the room. He didn't just admire her beauty—though her potent attraction was certainly part of what he felt—he admired her spirit. He didn't need to be told that her circumstances, not to mention the presence of the three of them, were probably very intimidating, yet she had taken his advice from their first night together and was making the best of the situation.

In truth, he was a little confused himself. Yes, he was glad she was bent on enjoying herself rather than feeling forced and used. The trouble was, he uncharacteristically wished she were enjoying herself only with him.

Never in his life had he felt possessive over a female.

Only three days since she'd been delivered and he'd already decided he would petition to be the one to breed with her. The fact he had influence meant almost surely his request would be granted, and he could keep the resulting child if he wished.

He had a feeling he would.

If he lived past the landing at Septinium. Ever since they had boarded the ship he'd had disturbing dreams, nightmares like he hadn't endured since he was very young and his parents were killed in an explosion. The sense of foreboding was strong and it had him worried. The future, usually so crystal clear, was full of shadows.

Jerra sighed and stirred in her sleep.

He ached to go to her suddenly. Not to make love to her, but to simply lie there and hear her breathe. It was a unique desire, and it startled him.

"You can't sleep?"

He glanced up from his brooding observation and saw Ian had come out of his room. He'd showered away the musk of lovemaking and wore a black robe that suited his coloring. Running his fingers through his damp hair, Ian dropped into a nearby chair and followed the direction of Ran's gaze. His normally hard expression softened. "I wore her out, I think."

Ran smiled with a little effort. "I think so, too."

"You were right. She's exceptional. I came so hard, I was afraid she would overflow. That hot little pussy is remarkable, though."

"Jerra was afraid she would fail you after pleasing Larik and myself. Since we all treat her well and don't make her feel like a slave or a whore, she wants to give back. I find it endearing, and quite frankly, arousing. Then again, just looking at her seems to give me an erection."

"Did you have to go jack off like Armada the other night?" Ian looked amused. "You could have joined us. I don't mind sharing."

He'd thought about it, but the trouble was, *he* minded sharing, which was a bit disturbing. When she was in his arms, he didn't want her attention on what anyone else might be doing to her delectable body.

"No, I'm saving it for tomorrow." Ran drained his wine glass. "She still has a lot to learn. For instance, that not only can a male lick a woman's pussy, but a female can lick and suck a cock."

"I have yet to taste her, and I look forward to it, but having her sweet mouth on me would be like a fantasy come true, and no pun intended."

They both chuckled, and in the resulting silence, Ran murmured impulsively, "I want to be the one to impregnate her. I thought you should know, since I intend to go ahead and petition now."

For a moment, Ian was quiet, his gaze still on the window. "I sensed something special with the two of you the minute you touched her. Is this something you see, Ran?"

"Yes…well, maybe. I'm having a little trouble with clear visions right now."

"Maybe?" Ebony brows shot up. "With you, there are usually few maybes. Are we talking about Septinium?"

"You feel it too, don't you?"

Very slowly, the other man nodded, his dark eyes unreadable. "I have a bad feeling in my gut. Death. It's as if I can smell it. I don't have your damned gift and I am glad of it, but I have good instincts when it comes to battle and it is as if a cold finger is running up and down my spine."

"That same skeletal finger invades my mind."

"We shouldn't go."

"No, probably not. There *will* be death. The question is ours or theirs."

"Theirs, certainly." Ian looked grimly certain. "Even if we perish to the last man, theirs also. It's a promise."

"A dark as hell one."

"This is a dark mission."

"Except for the girl." Ran gazed at her lovely face and the graceful lines of her half-nude form. "She's an unexpected ray of light."

"You want to breed with her, so I'd say you certainly do feel that way." Ian cocked a brow. "What would happen if one of us also wanted to father a child with our lovely human?"

"You would have to wait your turn."

"You wouldn't object?"

"I am not allowed to claim her completely, you know that. Just the child." By law, she belonged to the government. Her body could be loaned out for breeding, but with children born to captives, the babies were always put in the care of their S-species fathers. The mothers could be bred again to anyone who submitted for a human carrier and was approved.

"She couldn't carry my child." Ian said it with quiet practicality. "I was so large my S-species mother had difficulties. As it is most crossbreed offspring average close to twice the size of a normal human child and the females have to give birth surgically. Even if their remarkable vaginas could stretch enough, their pelvic area isn't designed for our size. I would never consciously endanger her life."

Ran recalled clearly how slim her hips had felt in his hands, but the system had been in place for decades and most females carried the babies without too much trouble. "I am only average in height and weight for our kind. In my case, she and I should be able to breed successfully and without danger to her."

"And so quickly you have decided you want her to be the one to share your genes?"

"Yes." It wasn't easy to explain, so he didn't try, but let the confirmation stand alone. "I'll send the official request tomorrow. The doctor can reprogram her microchip on the journey home."

After her capture and the subsequent physical examination and tests necessary to make sure she qualified for both sexual service and breeding, Jerra had a microchip inserted in her back just below her shoulder blade on the left side. The device controlled her hormonal levels to make sure she did not conceive during the course of her duties, or menstruate, which would be inconvenient. The embedded chip was permanent and would be used throughout her life to control her fertility. It could be reprogrammed in seconds, and when the mission was completed, she was already scheduled to be switched into a breeding cycle on their way home.

Ian still gazed through the window. "Wait until we're close to home to get her pregnant, if you don't mind. I'm sure Larik feels the same way."

Ran smiled wryly. "I thought somehow you both would ask me to delay the period when you wouldn't have any accessibility."

"Hell, yes." Ian chuckled. "How could you blame us?"

Since he had never enjoyed sex so much, he understood their point of view.

He couldn't wait to see her start to swell with his child. During gestation, he was the only male allowed to be with her, and he intended to make the most of that time.

If he lived to see it.

Chapter 5

The corridor was long, the lighting subdued, and Jerra felt a little self-conscious as she walked along. One on either side, Ran and Larik flanked her much smaller stature, and behind her, she could feel Ian's massive presence as he followed.

As an escort, she supposed it was probably fairly impressive.

She heard the music first, a faint wash of sound in the normally oppressive silence of the big ship, punctuated by a hint of laughter. When Ran scanned through and the door opened, she saw the large crowded room with a feeling of trepidation, but he took her arm and urged her through, and she stepped inside.

Instantly, almost everyone in the room scrambled to their feet, staring at her.

No, she realized, not at her, but behind her to where Ian towered over her diminutive human height. He said coolly, "At ease."

They relaxed, sank back down, and that was when their interested stares actually transferred to her. Through the sea of males, her entourage led her to a table and politely waited as she sat down. Immediately, a waiter arrived with several bottles and glasses, and slowly, the conversation and music resumed.

When they had suggested she hadn't left the room in weeks and asked if she cared to accompany them to the recreation area, she had jumped at the chance. But she hadn't thought about the fact it would be mostly soldiers, or that everyone would be curious to see the human female who was assigned to please the three most important men on the ship.

"Everyone is looking at me," she muttered, taking a sip from her glass.

"Of course." Ran looked amused, the low lighting gilding his chestnut hair and handsome face. "Males like to admire lovely females and you are more noticeable than most."

"We're showing you off," Larik informed her with his irresistible grin. "It's a bit arrogant of us, I suppose."

"My officers claim I'm more relaxed than usual." Ian poured himself a glass of the sweet wine she had grown to like. "Now they will know why."

"Why aren't there any other women here?" She glanced around, still saw she was the center of attention, and flushed.

"There are a few S-species female officers." Ran looked bland, lounging in his chair as he gazed at her. "The captives don't normally have time to relax often. Remember, there are only three of us and we keep you busy enough."

It was true. She rarely had much time to herself and though she had lost track of the passing days, Ran had told her they had been out now two of the three months it would take to get to their destination.

"You said it was getting monotonous to stay in our quarters all the time." Larik generously filled his glass.

She had, but, despite the unfamiliar music playing and the clink of glasses and low hum of voices, it was still another room filled with men who looked at her with only one thing in mind. "I admit I didn't expect to be of such interest."

"Speaking of female officers, here comes Liale, Colonel." Larik looked past her shoulder, and Jerra fought the urge to turn and look, held in place by the sudden change in Ian's expression. After months of sharing quarters, meals, and her body with each one of them, she had begun to know them quite well individually.

She hated to admit Lieutenant Herad was right about anything, but she had grown to feel honored to be chosen for the assignment given to her. Though they were not at all the same, her three lovers were all inherently *nice*, in and out of bed. They enjoyed her, but truthfully, only with the provision she enjoyed them, too. The giving of pleasure was a mutual journey, and she was not just the convenient receptacle for their lust.

In her mind, she had categorized them more than once. Larik was completely intellectual, yet constantly irreverent, and he considered sex light-hearted play, often tickling and teasing her, and they laughed together frequently even in bed. They had become fast friends also in a platonic way, and played games in the afternoons, usually squabbling over the results. He loved to make the most outrageous sexual wagers on the outcome, and she had learned to not press her luck, for with his mathematical inclinations, he could figure the odds and bet with uncanny accuracy.

Ian Helm was the opposite, serious, straightforward, and extremely capable. He rarely smiled, but she found when he did, it was compelling and lightened his normally stern expression. As a lover, he was careful, surprisingly gentle for such a large man, and often he liked to indulge in long periods of foreplay before the actual act of sexual intercourse.

As for Ran Kartel…well, Jerra found she thought of him the most, and knew a different excitement and enjoyment in his arms. He was naturally sensitive due to his special gift, and she experienced not only heightened pleasure when they made love, but also an almost disturbing sense of belonging. The way he kissed and held her made her feel not just wanted, but cared for, and she had the dismaying feeling she was falling in love with the handsome diplomat even though she tried to maintain a neutral distance. There was something about his self-assurance, his quick, seductive smile, and the weight of the responsibility he wore so easily that made him fascinating to an unsettling degree.

"Mind if I join you?" A female voice, husky but unquestionably higher in pitch, interrupted her reverie, and Jerra glanced again at the sudden impassive expression on Ian's face.

Ran nodded. "Hello, Captain Liale. Please, have a seat."

"Thank you." The new arrival sank into a vacant chair. She was like most S-species and very tall, probably almost as tall as Ran and Larik. Shoulder-length honey-colored hair brushed her shoulders and she had crystalline gray eyes. Her uniform tunic did not hide the fact she was statuesque in build, not just her height, but in her impressive breasts and the full flare of her hips.

Jerra was not gifted with any modicum of Ran's talent for reading the emotions of others, but in this case, she did not need it. The S-species officer looked at her and it was easy enough to read the emotion in her crystal clear eyes. Since the dislike couldn't be personal, Jerra assumed it had something to do with one of the males sitting at the table with them, and it was not difficult to guess which one.

Ian cleared his throat, but it was Ran who said quickly, "This is Jerra, Captain."

The female officer smiled, but there wasn't much warmth to it. "Yes, I know. She is rather hard to miss by both her attire and the staring eyes directed this way. Who can blame them, I suppose, for it isn't everyday one of the human females is brought into the officer's recreation area. In fact, it never happens."

Larik murmured in his easy way, "There isn't a rule against it, though."

"No." Captain Liale inclined her head and accepted a glass from one of the silent but efficient waiters. "I suppose there isn't, though this particular one might cause a small riot. They tell me she isn't surgically altered in any way. It is a bit hard to believe with those tits."

"I am sitting right here." Jerra kept her voice mild, but she wasn't about to be discussed like an inanimate object. "I'm pleased to meet you, Captain. It's pleasant to see another female after being surrounded exclusively by males so far this journey."

The show of spirit made the beautiful captain finally meet her eyes. "I am sure it has been quite a...*trial.*"

Ian blew out his breath at the silky sarcasm in her tone and his eyes glittered. "Captain."

The word was a warning, and Liale smiled thinly before picking up her drink and taking a sip. "Don't worry, I will behave myself, Colonel. I was merely commenting on her exceptional beauty, but it isn't necessary, is it, for you have already noticed."

Jerra glanced at Ran uncertainly at the acid tone of the comment, but he seemed more amused than anything, and so did Larik. It was Ian who looked profoundly uncomfortable, and she never would have thought to see his normal formidable composure shaken.

It was her turn to have her composure rattled because Ran reached over and took Jerra's hand, twining his fingers with hers and—very publicly—lifting it to his lips. He gently kissed her fingers. "I've certainly noticed."

It seemed like the hum of voices faded away as Jerra looked into his green eyes and all at once, she felt completely breathless. The affectionate gesture also seemed to take the jealous captain by surprise, for she suddenly found a great interest in her drink and she looked away.

If Jerra hadn't already been in love with him, she would have fallen into that particular abyss and gladly at the soft light in his eyes.

God help her...she was lost.

Though they had barely just arrived, he stood then, and since he still held her hand, pulled her to her feet. "We're going back."

Larik laughed, his blond hair gleaming in the subdued light. "I take it Ian and I need not rush our evening."

"Stay out as long as you like." Ran grinned back. He inclined his head. "Good evening, Captain Liale. I'm sorry to leave so abruptly, but—"

Dryly, she interrupted, "I think I understand your sudden urge to depart, Ambassador." She glanced at Ian, and for a moment, her expression was full of unguarded longing. "Believe me, I understand."

* * * *

What was it about her?

It was too much to try and decipher their lovely captive's intangible draw, but it existed, and over the past month, he had found himself sinking deeper and deeper.

Sinking deep, yes. It was exactly what he wanted to do. Between her legs, in the wet, hot heat he knew would consume him with perfection. Maybe it was the news he'd received that morning, but he felt a sexual hunger like he never remembered.

"My legs are not as long as yours. Can we slow down a little?"

The amused but very real protest made Ran realize he was striding down the hallway and practically dragging Jerra with him. Her scantily clad body looked small and graceful in the artificial light, and he wondered why the hell he'd ever thought he would be comfortable letting a battalion of soldiers gawk at her near nakedness. Sharing her with Larik and Ian was hard enough. He slowed down and abruptly swept her up into his arms. "Sorry. This will be faster."

"Ran!" The protest was said in a breathless laughing voice, but she pressed seductively against him and he could feel the voluptuous fullness of her soft breasts against his chest through his tunic. Her azure eyes were veiled by thick lashes, but he caught the gleam of excitement in those entrancing depths. The thin short dress she wore barely covered her luscious body anyway, and as he carried her through the hallway, she tugged it down as best she could over her thighs.

When the door to their quarters opened, he took her inside and straight into her room. Without much finesse, he deposited her on the bed and stripped off her gown. Full ivory breasts quivered enticingly with her quickened breathing and she watched him jerk off his clothes with a small smile on her soft mouth. Her lissome nude body was all pale curves and inviting shadows, especially the apex of her long slender legs, and he couldn't wait to touch and taste every inch of her. What's more, because he sampled her unequalled sexuality this past month as often as he could, he knew she was just as eager and probably wet and ready as hell.

His cock, already fully hard, stiffened further as he got in bed and pulled her against him. As they kissed, he rubbed the stiff length against the soft plane of her smooth stomach and groaned against her mouth. Ran rolled over to his back, moved his mouth to the sensitive hollow below her ear, and whispered against her neck, "Suck me, Jerra. I need relief before we can even start."

Obligingly, she started to scoot down the length of his body, but he caught her arms. "No." His voice was raspy with sexual arousal. "Like this."

He urged her into the position he wanted, lying on top of him face down the opposite way, her legs parted so her delectable pussy was visible. Letting his hands rub her ass, he could smell her arousal and his nostrils flared slightly at the same moment he felt her small hands caress his engorged penis and the first swirl of her tongue over the head. Usually, he liked to watch as she took him in her mouth—the sight almost as exciting as the exquisite heat and suction—but this way, with her golden hair spilling over her graceful back and the wetness of her open pussy against his chest was good, too.

Really, really good.

Too good, actually.

Jerra stroked his balls and the base of his shaft as she ministered to the tip of his cock and as much of the length as she could take. He could feel the pressure of the back of her throat as she slid downward, and see the up and down motion of her head. A low growl came from his chest. The pleasure of it was so much. The heat of her mouth, the brush of her tongue, and the skillful stroking of her hands worked him quickly into a fever pitch, and at the very last second, he wrapped his hand in her long hair and tugged her upward. His discharge was too much for her to swallow without choking, and he never came in her mouth. He groaned as he felt the rush of ejaculation rise through his pulsing cock and spurt out of him, covering her breasts and torso. She continued to stroke his flexing cock until he began to soften, and Ran could feel the warmth of his semen slick and slippery between their bodies.

"You have such a beautiful ass." His hands ran over the mounds of her buttocks, teasing the crack, and finding the small puckered hole there. He felt a fleeting moment of regret that the one thing he could never do with her was penetrate her anally with his cock. He was simply too big for her tiny orifice, but since there were a myriad of other pleasures they could give each other, the regret was only that. Extremely fleeting.

"Bring this a little higher, sweetheart." His fingers slid lower and found the wetness of her pussy, just tracing the seam of her labia. "I crave a taste."

As usual, Jerra did not need much urging. Like most females, she loved oral gratification. She wiggled backwards the necessary distance, his discharge making her slide easily, and Ran lifted her hips so she was on her hands and knees above him and her pussy poised over his waiting mouth.

"So pretty," he murmured, parting the soft, moist folds with his long fingers and seeing the vulnerable pink tissue beneath. The small bud of her clitoris in its protective sheath looked slightly swollen already and he reached out the tip of his tongue and lightly teased it.

Her reaction was immediate. She shuddered and murmured his name in a way that was an unmistakable plea.

"A little lower," he told her and she obediently opened her legs wider and sank down so his mouth was in direct contact with her heated center. She tasted divine as he skillfully began to bring her climax with his lips and tongue, and he savored her sexual fluids. Different from the S-species females he usually took to bed, her juices were sweeter, like honey and woman. Making love to her was different too, and it wasn't just the tantalizing tightness of her warm pussy, or her matchless beauty and responsiveness. Maybe it was the way she managed to be both captive and seductress without surrendering anything of herself she did not want to give. Just earlier, he had seen her challenge Captain Liale for treating her like an object. She wasn't one, and refused to be thought of that way.

Maybe that had been the moment he knew he had to take her back to their quarters because he couldn't wait to feel that same fire in bed.

Or maybe it was the way all the men in the room wanted to fuck her and he resented the hell out of it and wanted to whisk her away and keep her for himself.

That was the trouble. He wanted to keep her for himself. Forever. The realization made his hands tighten on her hips and for a moment, he went still, arrested by the notion of permanent possession.

Jerra moaned and moved in protest. "Please...please..."

Pushing the revelation from his mind, he concentrated on giving her what she wanted, knowing from the way she reacted as he lightly pushed his tongue into her pussy, she was close. When he stimulated her clitoris by sucking on it with gentle pressure, she went over the edge and cried out as her slim body tensed and began to shake in open carnal release.

She sank down on his chest finally, as if her arms could no longer hold her. For a while they stayed that way, and Ran waited for her to recover, content with stroking the elegant curve of her spine. He could tell the moment she noticed the returning swell of his erection for she slightly raised her head and gave a muffled laugh. "You have admirable stamina, Ambassador."

"I'm inspired." The promise was made in a light-hearted tone, but he wanted to make love to her. Face to face, so he could kiss and hold her as they reached for the ultimate pinnacle together.

* * * *

There was something different, but she couldn't quite figure out just exactly what it was. From the moment Ran had taken her hand and lifted it to his mouth in front of a crowded room, the gesture so gallant and reverent she was almost moved to tears, she had sensed a subtle shift.

In power.

Before, she had none. It had been made clear to her from the moment she had been taken and put on the ship. She'd been forced to give up her family, her clothes, her body, and most of all, her freedom. Confined and helpless, she'd done everything possible to make the best of her fate, and it had worked to a certain extent. Her only true resentment of the current situation was the fact she still had no say in her future.

Perhaps it would be better to worry about that when she wasn't sprawled on top of Ran Kartel's splendid muscular body with his cock lengthening before her eyes. Jerra reached out, closing her hand around his impressive length and squeezing gently. She traced the line of his stiffening penis with her fingers, and cupped his balls. They felt heavy and full, and if the evidence of his very recent climax wasn't spread all over the upper part of her body, she would have never thought he'd come not long ago.

There was something to be said for S-species men. They truly were Superhuman when it came to sex. All three of her lovers could regain an erection in a very short time and she had been informed it took an ordinary human some time to recover from orgasmic release.

"On your back." Ran easily moved her so she was supine and he adjusted himself over her. It was both habit and instinct to automatically spread her legs, and he settled there naturally as he leaned down and nibbled on her lower lip with just the slightest playful pressure of his teeth. His eyes closed as he prodded her vaginal opening with his cock, and Jerra took in a long breath and relaxed her inner muscles like she had learned to do in the past weeks. The conscious act eased his entry, but she found each time, she still was amazed at how disparate in size they were and yet could come together with such acute pleasure.

Aflame with the rush of her desire as she felt him ease inside her, Jerra ran her hands up and down the bunched muscles of his back. "You feel immense," she whispered, lifting her knees to give him complete access to her willing body.

"And you feel…perfect." His eyes opened as he slowly pushed toward total possession. "And so damned ready for me."

She was ready. Primed and ready from their mutual, earlier love play. And it was just as well. If experience served, they would spend most of the night in each other's arms. Of the three of them, Ran was most definitely the most demanding, insatiable in his need for her, and since she felt the same way about him, it was hardly a problem to accommodate his desires.

I love you.

The thought, which she normally tried to guard, or at least keep at bay by concentrating instead on the act of sex itself, sprang to her mind. To her dismay, she saw a reaction as his eyes narrowed and his inexorable advance halted. "What?"

"I didn't say anything." She quickly averted her gaze.

"You know you don't have to speak it out loud. Not with me."

She knew. That's why she consciously didn't allow anything but physical sensation to be in charge when they were together. To try and distract him and herself, she lifted her pelvis and tried to absorb more of his erection.

"Jerra." He didn't move to help, only half-penetrating her, his arms braced by her shoulders. "Look at me."

She shook her head, suddenly afraid. Of what, she wasn't sure, but definitely afraid.

"Look at me."

Finally, she obeyed, meeting his emerald eyes with defiant challenge, her heart feeling tight in her chest. "What?"

The set of his mouth was tense, as were the powerful muscles of his shoulders under her hands. "I would like to hear you say it."

A human captive in love with one of the most powerful males of the entire S-species? A male who manipulated nations and policies, who interfered in wars and held the ear of the entire government? It was ridiculous, and she knew it.

"No." Her refusal was decisive. "I won't, Ran. I think we both understand why."

Still unmoving, he smiled in a slow curve of his lips that made her breathing hitch to a higher notch. "You have the most damnable stubborn pride of any female—human or otherwise—I have ever met. And you are wrong, I don't understand. What's wrong with telling me?"

"Maybe because it's hopeless." She didn't want to feel anything but pleasure right now, and certainly not despair. "Just fuck me and forget it, please. I'm here and you can tell I'm ready for it, can't you?" She wriggled her hips, feeling the unsatisfying depth of only half his rigid cock.

"Stop trying to distract me." His expression was a mixture of tenderness and censure. "I want to talk about this."

"Now?"

"When better than when we are making love?"

Flippantly, she said, "I thought we were fucking."

"Then you were wrong. Have I ever used that word once in front of you? Even in the beginning, I have never referred to what happens between us that way."

In retrospect, he hadn't. Larik did often enough, but to him, sex was a game, and even he used the crudity only to tease her.

"No," she admitted.

"Is that what you feel I do to you?" His verdant eyes were dark, and his mouth a little tight. "Just use your body so I get off? Admit it, Jerra, from our very first time, you knew that wasn't true. Now, tell me."

He was right. He'd been sinfully tender, giving generously as well as taking, and the culmination of any woman's romantic dreams as a lover. Handsome, intelligent, sensitive, and solicitous; the list of his attributes went on. They all treated her more as a friend than a mistress, but Ran most of all. No wonder she'd been supremely foolish and tumbled into her current state. Inexperienced and alone, it was naïve for her to have dreams of forever, but maybe a romantic fantasy wasn't so surprising. At least she was pragmatic enough to realize it was just that—a fantasy.

But it didn't stop her from loving him.

"Fine." She said the word with quiet resignation. "I love you. I'm surprised you haven't sensed it before, but I've been doing my best to keep it hidden."

"I *have* sensed it before."

"There, you see, so why did you make me say it? Can we please just continue?"

"Yes, we can. In a moment." He stared down at her, holding her gaze. His thick hair was ruffled attractively against his strong neck and his muscular, bare torso glistened in the soft lighting. "First, I have something to tell you. I asked to be the one to inseminate you on our return voyage. This morning, my request was granted. I'll father the child you are scheduled to breed."

Jerra felt a burst of joy, for she had been apprehensive over the event she knew was destined to be initiated once they were headed back to the home planet of her captors. Larik was frank with her on any subject she cared to discuss, and the way he described the process made her feel both cold and nervous. She could be shuffled off to some unknown male, for the sperm donor had to want to breed with a human, and be responsible for the resulting child.

Slaves—like her—did not get to keep their children.

At least Ran would have theirs and she would know the child would be safe in his hands.

His face blurred as her eyes filled with tears and she felt the warm rivulets run down her cheeks. "Oh, Ran."

"Don't cry." With the pad of his thumb, he brushed her wet cheek. "That means we will have most of the next year together, Jerra."

"I know. Do you have any idea how relieved and happy I am?" She gave him a watery smile and touched his face, tracing the sensual curve of his lower lip. "Now, make love to me. I want to feel you all the way inside me."

At last, he obliged her and slid forward until she was fully impaled with his glorious length. It always felt good, but this time it was a heightened experience, and when he began to withdraw and sink back into her, Jerra felt a fierce elation that was both physical pleasure and emotional relief.

It was only a reprieve, she knew it, but a year was a long time.

As usual, she climaxed first, easily, her body arching into a long thrust as the erotic joy of it exploded in her brain, her nerve-endings, and centered between her legs. Ran didn't stop but continued to stroke his large cock in a carnal rhythmic motion into her pussy, and before long, she felt the contractions begin again. This time, he went with her, a guttural groan coming from his throat as he stiffened and his seed spilled in a forceful flood that coated her inner walls and filled the mouth of her womb.

Replete, she lay in his arms afterwards as he kissed her with slow, rapturous movements of his tongue and lips. They were both sticky with his sperm, and she was filled with it also, the warm liquid seeping from between her legs in decadent evidence of their lovemaking. He carried her to the cleansing room and they showered together in the warm spray, washing their bodies of the residue, touching, kissing, and whispering to each other. He took her there once more, holding her in his arms, her legs wrapped around his lean waist as the water flowed over their joined bodies and they came together again.

Her happiness might be temporary, but Jerra refused to think about it as she rested against his broad chest and felt the mutual wild beating of their hearts.

* * * *

Ian watched as Armada rose and left the table to join a group of engineers nearby. He gave an inward curse at being left alone with Liale. Larik could have a little more loyalty, but maybe the tension was making him as uncomfortable as it made Ian.

"Don't bother to conceal your feelings, Colonel." The words were said sarcastically and in a low tone.

He glanced over and pretended to not understand. "What do you mean?"

"Oh, please." Captain Liale's long perfect fingers smoothed her glass. "Your scowl could melt the inner core of Minoa. You don't want me here."

"You know, Captain, you have a very forthright approach, especially since I'm your commander."

"The trouble is, Colonel, you don't scare me the same way you intimidate everyone else." Her gaze was level and fearless.

"Is that so? I could order you to go." Ian growled the words, knowing he would never say them. Despite his resolve, his gaze dropped to the swell in the front of her tunic. By the stars, the woman had glorious breasts.

He wished he didn't know firsthand what he was missing.

"You avoid me."

There was no denying it, so he didn't. "Yes."

"Why?"

Giving her an exasperated look, he drank from his almost empty glass and said nothing.

She leaned forward a little, her blond hair, regulation length, at her collar, her lovely face set. "Are you sitting there thinking about what you are going to do to your pretty little human when you return to your quarters, Colonel? Tell me, how does such a slender small female manage to handle your immense cock? I've seen it at full attention, remember?"

He remembered, that was the trouble. Her obvious jealousy was flattering, but not what he needed at the moment. "What I do with Jerra isn't your business, Captain."

"The men talk about how good it is with the Earth captives. Certainly Kartel seems to think so for it was pretty obvious exactly why he dragged her off so quickly. The girl barely had a chance to sit down."

"You saw them. There is a unique bond there. I'm sure they'll spend the night enjoying the hell out of each other."

Her brows were a darker shade than her honey hair, and she lifted them a fraction. "So you will be alone tonight? It needn't be that way."

"You know the rules, Kia." The words came out fiercely and he almost stood up and walked away from the table. Almost. But somehow he couldn't quite do it, for if he couldn't have her, at least he could be near her. "I'm not just protecting myself. We'd both be fools to risk it again."

"I know. But I'm still willing." Though normally she was cool and professional in every way, and an ideal soldier with her natural air of competency and resolve, her mouth trembled just slightly as she spoke. "Does it tell you something about how I feel, Ian?"

It did, for she was also a career soldier. He shook his head, but his gaze locked with hers. "We can't."

Through the music and hum of voices, no one could hear what they were saying anyway, but she suggestively dropped her tone. "Follow me to my quarters in a little while. I'll be waiting, naked, wet and ready for you. Remember, with me, there is no need for restraint. I can take all of you in any way you wish to have me. Yes, I am sure your beautiful captive gives you pleasure, but does she give you passion? I can give you both, and you know it."

It was true. With Jerra, he had to be very careful and gentle. Her lovely responsive body accommodated him, and he thoroughly enjoyed every minute they spent in bed together. But he had fallen for the off-limits captain long before Jerra had been assigned to them. In bed, Kia was a match for him in every way, and her aggressive approach to lovemaking really turned him on.

She liked it a little rough, fast, and hard—and she was exactly right, she was passionate as hell.

His treacherous cock swelled, but he said firmly, "No."

She stared into his eyes as if oblivious to the crowd around them. "I'll be waiting."

"I won't come," he said, not at all certain he was telling the truth.

Liale gave him a slow smile and stood. "Yes, you will. We'll both come, Ian. Think about it."

Damn the woman. He watched her walk away, admiring the shape of her ass, and fought the urge to jump up and put his fist through the wall. Or maybe use his rock hard dick instead. He was embarrassingly aroused so quickly, he couldn't believe it. Normally, he would go back to their berth to Jerra and take care of it. After all, she was there for that purpose, but things had changed in the past few weeks. He didn't have to be told—neither did Larik—that their lovely roommate and the ambassador had moved beyond a purely sexual relationship. One had to only watch them together, in and out of bed, to see the emotional connection. It made him feel guilty now if he wanted her, and if he could satisfy himself in another way, he would.

He *could* actually.

With the female he really wanted.

Fuck!

The minute he shoved himself to his feet, he knew he would fall from grace and fall hard. Yes, he wanted to honor the strict guidelines that governed his job, including those that stood in place to make sure senior officers did not get involved with their subordinates. He understood the risk of feeling more for one of his soldiers than the others, and how it could compromise tactics in battle.

The trouble was whether he went to her or not, he already felt that way. He would die to protect Jerra as he had promised her. He would die a hundred times to protect Liale, and that was just that. Abstinence wouldn't change it.

If anyone noticed his distraction as he left, he didn't care. Ian strode off and made record time as he navigated the long corridors and lifts, the image of Kia, nude and waiting, embedded so firmly in his mind, his cock ached with every purposeful step. There were few enough female officers that she had her own berth. He scanned in, his position as commander giving him access to any room on the ship.

The door slid up and his heart stopped for a moment.

The beautiful captain was true to her word.

He stepped inside, his mouth going dry as he surveyed the image of her nude, gleaming body on the all-too small bed. The single room was simple and compact, and it made the impact of her graphic, sexual pose all the more dramatic.

Kia's eyes glittered as she watched him step inside. Her long legs were spread suggestively apart, and her hands held her lavish breasts lightly, as if displaying their sumptuous fullness. It was temptation incarnate, just as she meant it to be.

She was wet in anticipation of his arrival. He could see the moisture glisten on her labia. Ian said roughly, "You win, Kia. I hope we both don't lose."

If she felt the same worry, she didn't show it. "I can't lose if you're inside me. Hurry, Ian."

Hurry did not describe the way he shed his clothes. Frantic was much closer. When he freed his cock, she sucked in an audible breath and stared at his rampant length. "Bring that here. You know I want it."

"Don't worry, you're going to get it, all right." It was almost a threat the way he said it, for his need was such he could barely breathe. She'd pushed him on purpose—and it had worked—now he was ready to push back. Into her.

A moment later he did. No tender words, no persuasive kisses, but instead he lowered himself between her open thighs and thrust his cock into her waiting pussy with insistent need.

She arched and gripped his ass, forcing him in all the way, her breathy exhale a hiss of pleasure and exultation. "Yes...just like that. I love how big you are. No one feels like this."

He didn't want her to think about any other male, and in response, he leaned down and took possession of her mouth, his tongue graphically plundering. Kia battled with him in predictable ferocity, cupping his head and tangling with him in a war for dominance as they rolled on the bed and almost fell to the floor.

It was so hot and he was so damned aroused, he had to move.

"Fuck me," she whispered against his lips. "Really hard, Ian. I like it that way."

Well…shit, he knew she did. It was what made her irresistible enough he could throw away half his life for a single night of pleasure. He slid backwards and surged forward deep, feeling her nails score his buttocks, marking him. His lower body pumped fast, giving her what she wanted, and she gave it back to him with the roll of her hips and the strong grip of her thighs.

Arms braced, he stroked inside her, and watched the transformation of her expression as her orgasm rose. Her face grew beautifully flushed, tinting the smooth skin, and the color of her eyes seemed to actually darken as she stared up at him. Low, sexy moans came from her throat, and her tight nipples brushed his chest as he pounded into her.

It was a damned good thing the berths were all soundproof for she screamed as she came, her body arching wildly. The grip of her pussy as it tightened around his cock sent a jolt right down to his balls. Ian let the giant wave of release crash down, no longer holding back, and the rapturous rush of sperm exiting his body made his eyes shut tightly and his muscles shake.

The downward spiral back to reality was gradual and he became aware he was sprawled on top of her body. Although she was tall and fit, he was still considerably bigger, and with a small apologetic grunt, he shifted his weight.

Kia laughed and peered at him through her long lashes. "Believe me, you have nothing to be sorry for, Colonel. On my part, I hope you aren't bleeding."

At a guess he was, for he could feel the stinging scratches on his back and ass. "If I am, I don't care." He could still feel small pulses ripple through his cock, the sensation acutely pleasurable.

No, she wasn't as exquisitely tight as Jerra, but he and Jerra weren't meant to be life partners, anyway. He had the unsettling feeling he and Kia were and they came together in a perfect fit. He'd known females in a sexual way since he was old enough to get an erection. The woman looking up at him with a confident, satisfied smile was different. She was his equal in many ways, and her audacity took him off-guard. She'd now managed to get him to forget duty twice, and he had a feeling it was going to happen again.

Ian stroked her cheek. "We'll arrive at Septinium in less than two weeks. Kartel has a bad feeling about this mission. I share it."

The feline-like contentment faded from her face. "If we can get a clean landing, we've enough soldiers to take control, don't we?"

"By all reports, yes. But this is a planet that frequently does not follow the rules. We have no idea if the information they have fed us on population and military installments is accurate. Scans show more organic forms than what we thought, though they deny taking slaves or hiding armies."

She frowned. "I don't like the sound of that."

"Neither do I." Ian eased his cock out from between her open legs and rolled to his back. He stared at the ceiling. "I don't want you to go with the diplomatic guard, Kia. I'm sorry. I know you thought it was your assignment, but things have changed."

Her reaction was predictable, for she shoved up on one elbow and stared at him. "What's changed? I'm a damned fine officer and my men expect to escort Kartel and the government emissaries off this ship and protect them. We're ready for it, Ian, believe me."

"I know you are. Your command will still go. I'm taking them. You'll stay onboard and help guard the vessel." His voice shifted to the implacable tone he used when issuing orders.

"Is this because I'm female? If so, you're violating regulations, Colonel," she said icily.

"It's because you're *my* female." He clamped one hand on her shoulder and pushed her back down on the bed. In a swift, fluid motion, he rolled on top of her lush form again. "And in case you haven't noticed, I'm breaking regulations right now because of you, Captain Liale. So don't spout official rules to me when my come is all over your thighs where it is definitely not supposed to be."

She seemed momentarily speechless and he grinned lazily. "What? No smart-assed comment? That isn't like you, Kia."

"*Your* female?" The comment was made breathlessly.

"I'm not this damned stupid for anyone else." He hadn't really lost his erection even after his forceful climax, and he rubbed his cock against her hip.

"I'll have to resign."

"I know. I'm sorry, but we can work out the details later. Besides, if we breed, you'd have to, anyway. Once officers become mothers, they have to take permanent leave, you know that."

Her hand came up and touched his face and her eyes looked luminous. "You wish to breed with me? I was afraid you'd ask to be the one to inseminate your beautiful little human." She made a rueful face. "I'm jealous as hell of her."

"I noticed, but in case you haven't been paying attention, Kartel applied right away for that privilege. Besides, I doubt she could safely do it for me. You, on the other hand, will have no problem carrying my child. I like the idea, though it has never occurred to me before to want to share my genes with any female."

"It has certainly never occurred to me to resign my commission for some arrogant male, either."

Ian's brows shot up. "Arrogant?"

"Immensely arrogant." She reached for his erect shaft, wrapping her fingers around the stiff length of it and making him suppress a groan. "Although I admit you might have cause to be proud of this, Colonel Helm. It's a very magnificent cock."

"I'm glad you think so. Care to test how much you like it again?" He leaned down and kissed her, and all dark thoughts of the upcoming landing at Septinium were banished.

Liale made a purring sound low in her throat. "Absolutely."

"Roll over." He wanted to see just how bold his passionate bedmate might be. She liked it on the edge, she liked it hard and demanding, but how far would she go? Not waiting for her to comply, he easily flipped her onto her stomach and ran his hands over the mounds of her ass. He parted her and rubbed a questing finger over the small puckered hole between her cheeks.

Kia quivered. "What are you doing?"

"I want you this way."

"In my ass?" As a solider, she was used to being blunt.

Ian stifled a chuckle. "If we're throwing caution to the winds, why not? Have you before?"

"No." Tousled blond hair moved across her shoulders. "I've never trusted any male enough for anal sex."

"Do you trust me? I think you'll like it, as a little pain with your sex makes you hot, Captain." As he spoke, his finger traveled lower, to delve into the slick heat of her pussy for lubrication. Then he smeared his sperm and her fluids over her rectal opening and eased his finger in to the knuckle. The small muscles of her sphincter clenched and then relaxed.

"Shit, Ian," she moaned into the pillow. "Your cock is too big if that's how your finger feels."

"I'll get you ready, don't worry."

He did so, inserting another finger, widening her as he probed, and then a third, convincing her body to accept him. His cock was already slick from intercourse and when he slid his fingers out and positioned himself, he rubbed the tip enticingly between her buttocks. "Tell me again how you can take me any way I want you."

"Do it." Kia arched so he prodded her harder.

He entered carefully, not wanting to hurt her, but to give her a new experience he was convinced, with her extraordinary audacity in bed, she would enjoy.

He was so right, he discovered.

As his rigid penis worked into her ass, his lover moaned.

Hell, yes, she loved it.

Chapter 6

Jerra paced across the room for the hundredth time and took in a deep shuddering breath, trying to stay calm.

The second explosion had been much louder and the huge ship actually shifted enough, she felt it.

Oh, God, what was happening?

She knew the diplomatic team had left that morning, for even if Ran hadn't been dressed in a different uniform, she would have been able to tell by the way he kissed her. His mouth had lingered on hers with a gentleness that had nothing to do with sexual need, and he held her so closely, she almost could not breathe. Ian also, had looked formidably grimmer than usual and she had heard enough discussion on the matter to know they were all worried about the success of trying to use persuasion to solve the Septinium problem.

Apparently, they had been right, for suddenly she could hear the rhythmic beeping of hundreds of alarms and the ship shuddered violently enough she was thrown to the floor. Shaken, she scrambled to her feet and fought a surge of pure unadulterated panic. If the ship was actually being attacked, what was happening on the surface of the planet itself?

Ran!

The opening of the door made Jerra whirl in relief, but her heart sunk when she saw the tall, blond female captain step inside. Her cool gaze grazed over Jerra's body and she smiled thinly. Kia

Liale said, "You aren't hurt. Good. The last hit was close to here. You'd better come with me, human."

"What's happening?" Jerra clenched her hands into fists and stared at the S-species female she suspected now kept Ian occupied most nights. "Where are they?"

"Down there. Now, let's go. Apparently someone will have my head if you are killed because I didn't move you someplace safer."

Down there. The simple explanation was no explanation at all. "Have you had communication? What is going on?"

"My job isn't to explain anything to you." Liale stalked toward her. "Come with me or I'll throw you over my shoulder and carry you out."

"Aren't you worried?" Jerra said defensively, but she stepped forward willingly enough. Anything was better than being trapped with her unruly fears alone.

For a split second, the captain's face showed bleak emotion. "Yes. But it'll do no one any good, whereas if I stay focused on my job, I can at least follow orders. Now, are you going to cooperate?"

"Yes." Jerra nodded, feeling at least a small measure of connection. She followed the tall officer outside the quarters and down the hallway, noting with dismay most of the lights now flickered and she could smell the acrid hint of smoke in the air.

They went down several levels, and Liale took her into a small berth with a single bed and austere pale walls. She pointed at the bed. "This is my room and more centrally located, so safer. Sit down, lie down, do whatever you want, human. I guess we are stuck here together, since my orders are to take care you aren't injured. Quite frankly, I resent the duty, but I've been trained to do what the commander wants."

Ian had ordered protection for her? Jerra said coolly, "It occurs to me, Captain, he ordered it because he also wants you in a safe place. Your jealousy is misplaced. It isn't me he's protecting."

Ian's lover looked at her with her crystalline eyes. "His cock has been inside you. It's pretty straightforward to me."

"It wasn't exactly my choice, which you know full well."

"I still resent you, human."

"That isn't exactly a secret." Jerra sighed, sat down on the bed, and pushed back a stray lock of hair from her cheek. "Ian hasn't touched me in a long time, if that makes you feel better."

"A little, yes." Liale's shoulders relaxed a fraction and she sank into the room's one chair. She added a moment later, "I hoped he hadn't, but wasn't sure. There are some things I am not allowed to ask. Thank you for telling me." She smiled then, the first glimmer of any warmth Jerra had seen. "Quite frankly, I could not picture how someone as large as Ian could possibly mate with someone so slender and delicate."

It was a personal subject, but then again, the topic of sex didn't embarrass her any longer. Jerra laughed. "Carefully, if you want the truth. Thank goodness the capsules exist to ease the differences in our respective sizes. When I first saw him, I was terrified."

Captain Liale looked at her with level contemplation. "Actually, I doubt that. For someone with no real physical defenses against us, you seem to have been able to manage very well, Jerra. Look at Kartel, one of our leaders, so taken he barely leaves your side, I'm told."

"I love him." Jerra wasn't sure why she confessed it to someone normally antagonistic to her, but the words tumbled out, anyway. Probably because she was so worried she would never again hear his laugh or feel his persuasive touch. "They are all considerate to me, which I would never have imagined, but Ran and I connected from the beginning."

"So Ian says. It's a pity really, for the ambassador cannot have you permanently."

"If you think I don't know that, you're wrong." She took in a deep breath. "I try not to think about the future too much, and right now, I would trade anything just to have Ran safe. My lost freedom and the conditions of my captivity seem insignificant when I am worried about his life."

The captain narrowed her eyes. "You do love him."

At that moment, the ship rocked again. Liale jumped up and was slammed into the wall by a second shudder, her tall form colliding with such force she seemed momentarily stunned.

Jerra found herself on the floor once more, a little dazed at being thrown so hard. A high-pitched whistle pierced her consciousness and she caught her breath and got up. "Are you hurt?"

"I don't think so, but someone is." Ian's lover looked grim as she rubbed her shoulder. "That alarm means we have casualties."

The thin sound was more unpleasant than ever now that Jerra understood its significance. "Where are you going?" she demanded as Liale scanned the door open.

The other woman said shortly, "The main bay. I'm guessing they are bringing back wounded from the surface. If they need help, it's my job to be on hand. You'll be safe enough here, human."

"I'm going with you." Jerra said it firmly, with no equivocation.

"No, you are not. You'll be a distraction and a nuisance."

"I'm a trained nurse."

Liale eyed her and there was a flicker of indecision in her expression. "Truly?"

"Yes." It was irritating to realize she was regarded as having no purpose, except the sexual one she had been selected for by her abductors. "Believe me, Captain, I had an existence before the S-species decided to take over my life. I wasn't just a nurse, but a surgical nurse."

"You're too young."

"No." She said it with gritty conviction. "Believe it or not, I'm actually very intelligent and was trained at an exceptionally early age. Now, shall we go?"

"I could get in trouble if I take you. I am not sure what Ian would want. I'm pretty sure he doesn't see past your pretty tits and that tight little pussy he's been in so often."

Jerra fought the urge to lash back, taking a deep breath. She gave the S-species female a level, steady look. "You are letting your jealousy affect your judgment, Captain Liale. If help is needed and I can give it, I am sure Ian would want me to be useful."

"Maybe so," she admitted grudgingly and glanced over her scanty attire. "I wish you were wearing something else. I can see your breasts almost as clearly as if you were naked. But maybe you can help." She gave a small grimace. "Besides, this way at least I am still keeping you with me like he wanted. Come then, but follow orders."

Grateful to be able to do anything besides sit and worry, Jerra nodded and followed her out the door.

* * * *

His side was on fire, his mouth tasted of soot and smoke, and he was bleeding everywhere.

He was still way better off than Kartel.

Shit! He'd failed.

Ian pressed on the welling wound in his friend's stomach and bit back the string of swear words he wanted to let loose. There was shrapnel embedded deeply from the explosion and Ran's breathing had gotten ominously shallow.

It was hard to imagine such vitality extinguished, but it was not impossible. Ian had been a solider long enough he'd seen plenty of death.

"Fuck, no," he muttered, his bloody hands slippery as he applied enough pressure to keep the ashen man lying so still from at least bleeding to death. "You aren't going to die, Kartel. No way. Stay with me." On an afterthought, he added, "Think of Jerra."

For a moment, he could swear his friend's eyelids fluttered.

If that was the way to keep him alive, he wasn't above exploiting it.

"She's so soft, isn't she?" he said in a persuasive whisper. "So warm inside, so tight and responsive. I see how she looks at you, and you told me how she loves you. If you leave her, she'll be fated to servicing other S-species males her whole life, and bearing children who will be taken away immediately. Is that what you want for her?"

Kartel gave a small groan, and despite his own wounds, Ian felt like leaping up and cheering. He went on, hope glimmering. "I think you could try and free her. No, it isn't done, but why not try? Petition the Council to see if they might gift her to you. It isn't like you haven't served Minoa in every way possible. When you pull through this, they are going to owe you for insisting we go instead of listening to your advice. They'll know it. Call in all your favors."

Ran opened his eyes, but his stare was unfocussed. "What…happened?"

Damn, he'd lost a lot of blood. The extraordinary pallor of his skin was frightening.

"They didn't give us a chance," Ian said, gratefully feeling the transport lock into docking mode. "The first bomb exploded before we even landed. They destroyed our craft and we crashed. From there, they started a full assault on the ship, keeping rescue at bay. Finally, I was able to get through with a few orders."

"What?" Kartel's green eyes held intense curiosity besides his obvious pain and weakness. Mangled and bloody, he seemed only half-conscious, but it was better than nothing.

"We took out the capital." Ian was no diplomat and he was not going to apologize for having a heavy hand. He'd recommended that strategy all along. "Most of their population and the full seat of their government. If they didn't expect it, they were fools. They cannot attack diplomatic S-species envoys. In my mind, if they didn't want to talk, that's just fine. We can deal with each other in a much simpler way."

"Simple?" Ran smiled, a ghost of the real thing curving his lips.

"Dead is simple," Ian explained succinctly. "No matter the race, everyone understands death. Most universally decline the honor."

"I didn't...want...that."

"I didn't, either. They did. You do peace. Let me handle war."

"You got it." His friend's eyes drifted shut, his pallor pronounced.

"Whoa. None of that. You aren't leaving, got it? Tell me, what do you see for our lovely Jerra? Surely you've had visions? Come on, stay here and we'll talk about it."

"She looks even more beautiful pregnant, but who knows if it is mine. I've been having some problems seeing clearly lately and we all know she is supposed to be bred."

"It's yours." Ian fought the tightness in his throat. "I feel it like I felt the ominous repercussions of this fucking misguided mission."

"Right now...she's frightened."

"I would guess. They've been blasting at the ship, but once we were clear and their main defenses eradicated, it should be quiet up there. Plus, Kia is with her."

"Kia is as frightened as she is."

Ian felt his mouth tighten. He said gruffly, "That isn't possible, Ran. She's a soldier. Trained, hardened, and experienced."

"She's in love. It changes the chemistry…of…everything."

Damned insight. Ian was infinitely glad he didn't have it. "We're here. Everything is going to be fine now."

"Is it?"

Ian said firmly, "Yes."

The doors opened and the first medical staff poured in. Ian saw them check visibly as they registered the severity of the injuries of the occupants of the craft, and he told the nearest doctor briefly, "Bomb."

The man nodded and dropped to his knees next to Kartel, shouting for assistance. Ian was shouldered out of the way and he reluctantly left his friend in more competent hands.

Moments later, he was glanced over by a young female doctor who apologetically pronounced his wounds superficial and left him for someone who needed her more. Unfortunately, there were plenty of those. Regardless of his rank, he handed over bandages, carried stretchers, and did whatever he could for his men.

When he first spotted Jerra, he thought perhaps he was hallucinating. She was bent over a fallen man, her small hands busy at work with what looked like professional competence as she dressed a wound, her long unbound hair like a golden curtain. Despite his injuries, the fallen solider was smiling and Ian really couldn't quite blame the young male. Considering the low cut front of her almost translucent dress, he probably had one hell of a wonderful view of her spectacular breasts.

If Jerra was there…

"You're bleeding, Ian." Liale spoke gruffly as she strode toward him, but her face was pale. Her eyes glittered as she scanned his myriad of cuts and scrapes. "Why aren't you being treated?"

"I'm told it is insignificant and I agree."

"It looks bad." She gestured at the blood dripping from his fingers.

"Take my word, it's just a few flesh wounds and forget it."

She muttered something about a stubborn male and he grinned for the first time since the explosion and crash, feeling a moment of light-hearted relief. "You have no idea," he informed her, just barely resisting the urge to throw his arms around her to kiss her soundly despite the melee of milling medical personnel.

"What went wrong?" She took the other end of a stretcher, lifting it with ease, her tall athletic body moving fluidly.

As they took the unconscious soldier toward the open bay of the ship, Ian told her, "Everything. They didn't exactly welcome us with open arms but hit the transport and we crashed. Then they began a full assault. Luckily, both Kartel and I expected trouble." He shrugged. "The craft behind us was full of the soldiers in your command, Kia. They are very well-trained men. My compliments, for they got us out quickly and efficiently."

She nodded, shouldering her way through the door. "They work well together. What of Septinium?"

"I would guess they now understand that when S-species send a request for peace negotiations, they should behave like civilized creatures. That last explosion was fall out from our retaliation."

"Where's Kartel?"

Ian had expected her to ask, for the tall ambassador was hard to miss. "On one of these stretchers somewhere, hopefully with a very competent physician in attendance. He's lost a lot of blood, I'm afraid."

"Jerra won't handle that well."

He lifted his brows. "You care how she feels?"

Kia scowled. "I didn't say I cared. I merely know how your beautiful little human feels about him."

"I told you if you gave it a chance, you might actually like her."

"I wish you'd never touched her, but you're right, she can stand up for herself, despite the fact she's a captive. I can perhaps understand why Kartel is so obsessed with her." Liale grimaced as they carefully deposited the stretcher on a nearby bench in the medical area. "Besides the obvious reasons, of course."

"She is beautiful." He couldn't resist making the comment for he loved Kia's combative possessiveness. It matched his own fierce desires.

"She says you haven't touched her in a long time." His lover immediately bristled and put her hands on her hips. "Was she lying to me?"

"No. In my experience, Jerra does not lie. It isn't her nature to be dishonest."

"Stop complimenting her."

"Is that an order? Let's not forget I am your superior officer, Captain."

She was predictably unfazed by the reminder. "I am your female. That means I am the only one you want in your bed. Forget your pretty little human, Ian. Besides, as far as I can tell, she belongs to Kartel."

Ian felt all urge to tease her melt away. "I only want you, Kia, you know that. As for Jerra and Ran, well, let's hope he lives so we can see what happens next."

* * * *

Everything was a haze. The pain, the sound, the coppery smell of blood, none of it made sense.

Except one thing.

A hand. One small hand, dwarfed by his much larger one, clasping his fingers.

Ran turned his head a fraction and his nostrils flared as he drank in her scent over the combination of other impressions assaulting his senses. He knew that fragrance better than anything in his universe.

Jerra.

He tried to whisper her name, but it came out instead as a low croak, and immediately someone slipped an ice chip into his mouth. She bent closer for he could feel the silky brush of her hair on his cheek.

"Hush, Ran. Stay quiet. The doctor took enough metal out of you to build a second ship."

It certainly felt like it, so maybe she was right.

Cool fingers touched his cheek. "Sleep and heal. That's another advantage of being S-species they tell me. You'll recover twice as fast as an ordinary human."

Recovery was an abstract concept. The only solid thing was the brush of her fingertips on his burning skin and the musical sound of her voice.

"Stay," he managed to mumble.

"As if I would ever leave," she said in tremulous whisper.

Contented, he drifted off.

Chapter 7

She really could not believe it, but the man had an erection.

Jerra said forcefully, "No."

"You're a very cruel nurse." Ran smiled at her from the bed, all lounging persuasive male. His bare torso still covered with bandages, but his long cock was decidedly erect beneath the sheet casually drawn to his waist. "I obviously need you. Can't you help me out?"

In exasperation, she shook her head. "You are hardly recovered enough for gymnastic sex, no matter what you think."

His green eyes held an undeniable smoldering heat. "I'll happily let you do all the work. Besides, I know for a fact they are still giving you the injections because you are scheduled to breed. I also know Larik and Ian leave you entirely to me, so you are as celibate as I have been lying in this damned bed. Tell me you don't want it, too."

He was right. She wanted him. But above all else, she wanted him *well*. It had been weeks since they started their return journey to Minoa and his recuperation coming along nicely, but whether or not he was ready to make love to her still hung in the balance. "I think it is a bad idea, no matter what I want."

"Aha. So you do admit you want this." He brushed down the sheet and touched himself, his graceful long-fingered hand running up the length of his impressive erection to the tip. Semen beaded on his finger.

"Yes." She wasn't going to deny it, but neither would she encourage him to do something that might impair his already miraculous recovery. "Desire should be separate from something that could be a damned bad idea, Ran."

"Sit on me. I won't even move if you insist."

She eyed him uncertainly, tempted but unsure. "If I hurt you, I won't forgive myself."

Triumph gleamed in his gaze. "You are less than half my size. How could you hurt me? Besides, you cannot let me lie here in this state all day. My balls actually hurt. Come on, take off your clothes and bring that glorious body over here. I'm going to bet you're already wet."

She *was* wet and hot between her legs, her pussy throbbing at the sight of his engorged penis. "Ran," she said in reproach, but did slip her dress over her head. Her nipples were already stiff with desire as she approached the bed. When she reached him, she consciously stayed just out of reach. "I still think this is a bad idea."

"*I* think it is a marvelous idea. Step closer."

His heavy-lidded gaze seemed to hold her prisoner and she did what he said, the command in his voice hard to deny. Immediately, he slid his fingers up her inner thigh and slipped two into her pussy, gently exploring and stretching.

She almost came right then.

Those damned shots. He was right. Taking the injections without any sexual relief was difficult. Jerra moaned and Ran laughed lightly. He thumbed her clit and she quivered violently.

"Climb up," he invited, removing his soaked fingers. "It's all yours."

She was careful as she got on the bed and straddled his hips. She grasped his cock and positioned the tip at her slit. As always, she had to gradually absorb the large width and length of his shaft, her body opening to accept it, her breathing shifting into a rapid pattern as she filled her vagina inch by inch.

It felt so good. So right. She loved him beyond what she believed was possible.

Ran's gaze was riveted on the joining of their bodies, watching as his cock slowly disappeared inside her. "Yeah, sweetheart, just like that."

When the tip nudged her womb, she began to climax. It was beyond her control, the pleasure so intense and so denied during his weeks of recuperation she shuddered uncontrollably and cried out in abandoned satisfaction. In return, Ran growled, "Yes."

His hands spanned her hips, pushing her downward and forcing himself deeper as he ejaculated. The copious amount of sperm seemed to pour into her forever, each flex of his release a hot spurt she could feel with amazing, vivid sensation.

"I needed that." He said the words with a dazzling smile, still firmly holding her in place impaled on his stiff penis. "Don't bother to get off because I'll want you right back here again in a moment. We'll slow things down this time if you don't mind."

It was encouraging to know he felt well enough to have his sex drive back, but she still worried over tiring him too much. "I want to please you, you know that, but promise me you won't overdo it."

"You do please me." His hands slid upward to her breasts. He began to stroke and fondle her, rubbing her nipples with his thumbs, cradling her flesh in his palms. "More than any female I have ever known."

As he had never said he loved her in return, desire was probably as close to that sentiment as she would ever get. She'd had plenty of time to think about the situation while she cared for him in the days since the failed mission. He was an important individual and it was demonstrated by how his injuries and possible death had caused a furor not just on the ship, Larik told her, but on their home planet.

A powerful S-species male did not become permanently attached to a human female slave, she needed to face it. However, if he enjoyed her enough, maybe he would ask to keep her for sexual service and she would be content.

Anything to stay with him.

"You please me, also." Her voice was soft and she looked into his emerald eyes.

"I like the idea of being your only lover." He rolled a taut nipple between his fingers with delicate precision.

Larik and Ian had also given her pleasure many times, but Ran was the one she truly loved. "I like it, too."

"The doctor told me this morning he has reprogrammed your chip so you will ovulate."

"Yes." The idea of his child growing inside her made her feel both joy and despair over the inevitable separation.

"Then we need to make a concentrated effort to impregnate you." Ran dropped one hand and with one skillful fingertip stimulated her clit. Almost immediately, she felt the flutter of orgasmic sensation deep in the pit of her stomach. He watched her face as he applied just the right amount of pressure, and beyond her will, her entire body began to tremble.

Jerra moaned her pleasure, her open thighs tightening around his hips, his cock stretching her deliciously wide. At his urging, she began to ride him, lifting up and sinking down on his shaft, the lubrication of her arousal and his discharge making the motion easy. True to his word, he did not move, except to encourage her with his hands.

When she climaxed again it was wild and abandoned, her throat arched back as the rapture of it slammed through her body. She felt his response as he pumped into her, his breath escaping in a long hiss of satisfaction.

"That's enough," she told him sternly when he protested as she climbed off his lean body. "You still need rest, Ran."

"You are a very bossy nurse, have I mentioned that?" The grumble was pure male. "Last I knew, I was the one with the authority."

"No one could force me to do anything to harm you no matter who they are."

"For someone who looks like an angel, you can be very fierce, sweet Jerra, and not just in bed." His laugh rang out, low and mellow.

It was all too easy to recall the heart-stopping moment when she had first seen him on the stretcher, covered in blood, his flayed skin and gaping wounds a horrifying sight.

"I love you," she said simply and reached for her discarded dress.

* * * *

Ian sat in a chair, dwarfing it with his size, his long legs extended. He said, "I've written my report and the Council has it. What they do now is up to them."

"My guess is they will consider it not as much of the disaster it was because your swift actions actually solved the problem. I doubt Septinium will be a future threat to anyone." Ran rubbed his jaw, glad to be out of his bed for the first time, just the mere fact of donning his clothes making him feel more like himself. They sat in the common room of their berth and he had actually felt like drinking a glass of wine.

"Or they might discipline me for taking such an aggressive approach."

"They might." Ran knew his government's opposition to being perceived as high-handed. "But I doubt it. Not with half of a diplomatic team dead and the other half wounded. They knew we wanted to negotiate a peaceful solution, but they wouldn't have sent you along if they didn't think it was possible it would not turn out that way."

Ian nodded, his dark hair brushing his neck. "True enough. I have other troubles, though. I suspect they know of my relationship with Kia. There is no way others on this ship do not suspect where I spend my nights and that I'm directly breaking the rules. She is going to resign, but that does not change the fact I've breached the code of ethics."

"I think you underestimate the loyalty of those who serve under you. I doubt anyone has reported it."

"If they have, though—"

Ran shook his head. "They don't know. Trust me."

His friend gave him a keen look. "You see this?"

"Yes. Besides, they would contact me for confirmation. After all, we share a berth."

Ian seemed to relax. "That's good to know. I never imagined I would ever do such a thing, but you know, she has a powerful effect on me."

"I do know." He couldn't help it, his gaze strayed to the window and the bed visible through the glass. Jerra napped often in the afternoons now that she was pregnant.

Ian followed his look. "Yes, I imagine you do know. Tell me, when will they let you know what is going to happen?"

"I am going to meet with the board as soon as we get back. Already, I have requests from several members for a face to face interview." Ran felt his stomach knot. "I hope you're right and they grant my request. The laws governing intermarriage are archaic and date back to the evolution. At the time, we were emerging into our own species and the separation of the genes made sense. But now we are deliberately breeding human genetic patterns back into our bloodlines. Surely, forbidding mixed marriages is based on a rule that is no longer necessary."

"There is a certain amount of snobbery involved, you know that, Ran. You are a public figure, an S-species hero, and for you to wish to mate with a human took them weeks to approve. Marrying her might be met with refusal. In their eyes, she is simply a slave and inferior, no matter how bright and beautiful."

He knew all of that only too well. "She helped save lives." He hoped the testimony of the doctors and the soldiers and others she'd worked on during that fateful return to the ship would aid his cause. "There was no obligation on her part to wish to help. Let's remember she was abducted for the purpose of sexual servitude. She owes us nothing, yet she gave freely, anyway."

"I am the last one to disagree with you on the point, and believe me, I will lend my weight to any argument you make." Ian idly fingered his wine glass. "Tell me, does she know?"

"That I wish to make her my life partner? No. As you just pointed out, it might not be possible, so why get her hopes up for something that hasn't been approved of for generations. If they refuse, I will settle for keeping her as my personal property. If they refuse that..." His voice trailed off as he contemplated having to let her go to be bred to someone else. Finally, he finished with quiet emphasis, "I am not sure what I will do. I see most things with clarity. For myself, it isn't as easy."

Ian nodded, his face set. "Who knew when we set out on this mission, it would so change our lives."

Ran smiled. "I didn't see how, but I knew before we ever set foot on this ship, things would never be the same for either of us. I believe I mentioned it."

"Yes, you did. I don't know if I should envy Armada for not having an emotional involvement with a female, or feel sorry for him. He's grumbled more than once about having to share one of the other humans in deference to your possession of Jerra, but I know he's also happy for you."

"His turn will come."

"Oh, really, will it? What do you see?"

"Chaos ahead for him. It has to be a female. What else causes so much confusion in our normally ordered lives?"

"Nothing." Ian said the word succinctly and drained his glass of wine.

* * * *

She was alone.

Truly alone. Locked away and forgotten.

Jerra stared out the window and saw the foreign landscape with a sense of fatalistic contemplation. When she had been escorted off the ship, somehow she had assumed Ran would come to her. Instead, she'd been taken to the room she now occupied, and despite her requests for information, told nothing about what was happening.

Gently, she pressed her hand over the subtle swell of her abdomen. The doctor had explained since S-species had larger children, she would show the pregnancy much faster and grow larger. Luckily, the babies needed a shorter gestation period and he had already given her the date she was scheduled to deliver.

And what happened after that?

No one seemed to know. When she asked Ran, he had simply kissed her and began to make love to her, the distraction obvious but an effective tactic. She had the distinct feeling he either didn't know himself, or didn't want to tell her.

Please don't let it be the latter, she prayed.

The door opened, startling her out of her abstraction. Jerra turned, her mouth parting in surprise as she saw Captain Liale step inside. Since they were hardly the best of friends—but had come to an uneasy truce in her opinion—she was both surprised and glad to see a familiar face.

"Hello, human." Liale tossed something on the small bed. "I've been sent to ready you though it's hardly a duty I asked for. Put that on. You can't go as you are."

"Go where?"

"Before the Council."

"What council?"

"I am not interested in explaining. If you don't get dressed right now, we'll be late and it won't help, believe me."

There was something about her tone that made Jerra stifle her urge to argue. She saw the garment on the bed was a gown made of some filmy—but thankfully not transparent—material, and as she picked it up, it flowed over her hands with a unique softness. The gold threads glimmered in the pale light of the three moons that hung in the sky outside her window.

Nudity no longer bothered her, not after living with a window open to practically her every movement, and she gratefully took off the translucent gown designed to display rather than conceal her body, and slipped on the one Liale had brought her. It hugged her curves but fell almost to the floor, at least not showing off every bit of her anatomy. She ran a brush through her long hair and turned around.

The tall captain looked at her with what seemed like actual approval. "Your beauty might sway them. Come, let's go."

"Sway them how?"

Liale made an impatient movement with her hand. "The governor has requested you be transferred into his care."

An icy lump seemed to settle in her stomach. "What? They can't. I'm pregnant with Ran Kartel's child."

"The Council can do whatever they wish, believe me, and he will get the child no matter what they decide. Now come."

She had no choice, as usual, but to obey. If she wanted, Ian's lover could easily physically force her because of her superior size, and she would just as soon preserve whatever dignity left to her.

Jerra followed her out, her palms damp, and they went to the same sort of small transport used to bring her to her latest accommodations. Liale refused to say anything more as they traveled across the teeming city and Jerra finally subsided into an uneasy silence.

The security measures required to get into the building they finally reached were complicated, but they seemed to be expected. Several of the S-species guards looked at her curiously and Jerra tried to keep an impassive expression. Once inside, Liale took her down a series of long hallways, past more guards, and finally into a huge room.

Cool air brushed her bare arms and she shivered. It was the size of a small amphitheater and she was led to the very center, where a semi-circle table faced a small dais. To her relief, she saw Ran amid the members who sat there, but her elation faded when she registered the impassive expression on his handsome face. There was no welcome in his green eyes and no emotion in the way he looked at her.

Her heart felt as if it plummeted through the floor.

Liale briefly saluted the panel and left with quiet efficiency.

"Jerra Aubrey?" One of them, older, with a dark beard and piercing eyes, spoke her name slowly.

"Yes." She nodded, feeling their unabashed scrutiny.

"The governor has petitioned to have you made his personal property due to the nature of your superior service during the recent mission. Normally, you must understand, once taken from Earth, you belong to the government of Minoa. The unusual request is currently under debate."

The governor? Not Ran?

She looked at him and still he simply sat there. She had known she would be passed on to other S-species males for breeding, but he had promised her they would at least be together for the period of her pregnancy. "What is it you wish from me?" she asked boldly, doing her best to look composed when what she really wanted was to burst into tears.

"Actually, I suppose we were more curious than anything." One of the others spoke out, his gray hair and regal bearing impressive. "I am told you insisted on helping after the wounded were brought back from Septinium. Tell us why if you will."

"I was hardly going to let anyone suffer if I could do something about it."

"But you are a slave," another one said.

She looked directly at the speaker. "Quite frankly, I have never felt that way. Yes, you captured me, forced me into sexual servitude, and have even bred me, but there are some things you simply cannot own. In my heart, I am free. When I give, it is of my choice. You can take all you wish, but the only thing of value is what is given. If you choose to force me to go to someone other than Ran Kartel, I suppose I can do nothing about it. However, rest assured they will never enjoy me as he did, for I love him and right now his child grows inside me."

The older gray-haired opened his mouth as if to speak, but then lapsed into silence. The bearded man spoke instead. "I see. Thank you, Miss Aubrey."

It was a dismissal, but she didn't move. Instead, she looked at Ran, hoping he would see the emotion in her eyes. "You are not going to fight for me in any way?"

"I have."

The resignation in his voice made her furious. "That's it? You would let me go so easily? I am not your slave, and you well know it. We are lovers. It is an entirely different thing."

"I agree." The ghost of a smile seemed to hover around his lips. "Entirely."

"I do not know who the governor is and I don't care. I will not be passed off—"

"Miss Aubrey, you are dismissed."

"I am *not* dismissed." There was too much entirely at stake for her to care about their high-handed rules. She was shaking, her unhappiness tangible and all consuming, and she clenched her hands into fists. "Perhaps you think you are superior, but I will tell you that isn't true if you do not let love and compassion govern your actions. It isn't simple, believe me, because I know firsthand the difficulties of gaining affection for someone who has complete and utter control over your life. But being powerless physically does not make you powerless emotionally. I do not care what you all decide. I will not—"

"Jerra." Ran stood up. "I am the new governor of Minoa."

His declaration stopped her rant. She stared at him. "What?"

"I am the new governor. I was just appointed. The Council is now trying to decide if the law needs to be changed so humans and S-species of either sex can marry legally upon my recommendation. So far, it is outlawed because your race is considered inferior." His emerald eyes glimmered in amusement. "I think, however, you just made quite a point on the subject."

Her knees felt actually weak. "I did?"

He left his position at the table and came around toward her. "Yes, you did. I don't believe there is anyone here who is in question over your feelings."

"Ran." She didn't even realize she'd moved until she felt his arms draw her close and she buried her face against his chest. "I have missed you so much."

He stroked her hair and laughed softly despite their audience. "I know. Believe it or not, as inferior as my passion might be to your human emotion, I do have a modicum of sentiment and I have missed you, too." He glanced at the Council. "Well? Have you made a decision?"

Epilogue

It felt like their first night together.

Jerra laid her son gently in the cradle. His extraordinary beauty always amazed her, but then again, she felt the same way about his father. Thanks to Ran, she had even been able to communicate with her parents several times, and he'd proposed a trip so she could let them see their grandchild as soon as he was old enough to make the journey. She quietly eased the door to the nursery open and slipped out.

"Is he finally asleep?" Ran waited for her in bed, propped on one elbow, the soft starlight outside the window illuminating his thick shining hair and brilliant eyes.

She nodded. "He was hungry."

Her husband smiled. "As far as I can tell, he is a voracious eater for someone so small. I'm a bit jealous for he currently gets to spend more time with your breasts than I do."

"They are free at the moment." She hadn't bothered to refasten her gown and saw his gaze glimmer as she walked toward the bed. Her breasts, heavier now since she gave birth, swayed as she moved. The doctor had confirmed it was fine now for her to resume normal sexual relations and she was more than anxious.

"I was rather hoping you might find a minute or two for me."

She shimmied out of her nightdress. "Are you really jealous?"

"Quite the contrary. Seeing you hold my child is the most moving experience I could ever imagine." His brows lifted.

"However, I won't bother to deny I want to make love to you. My erection kind of gives me away."

She teasingly lowered her lashes. "I think you will find me very cooperative and subservient, Governor Kartel."

He chuckled. "Subservient? That doesn't describe you, I'm afraid. From our very first meeting, I knew that. Now, come here and let's recall our initial introduction detail by detail. It seems to me we both enjoyed it very much."

Jerra slid into his arms. "You didn't give me much choice but to enjoy it as I remember it."

He rolled her to her back and settled his mouth against hers in a persuasive tender kiss. When he lifted his head, he whispered, "If there is one thing you've taught me, my love, is that there is always a choice. Lucky for me, I chose you."

She was the lucky one, she thought drowning in his next kiss, feeling his passion but also his love under the light of the pale stars.

PALE STARS IN HER EYES
The Starlight Chronicles

THE END

WWW.ANNABELWOLFE.COM

THE COVENANT

The Starlight Chronicles 2

Annabel Wolfe

Chapter 1

The request to switch to a military frequency was never a good sign. Larik Armada watched the screen to his left and saw the dots get larger and align themselves in an unmistakable formation.

The pilot glanced over, his mouth set in a grim line. "I think someone forgot to mention to me being escorted in by six fighters. They're directing us to a lock beam for docking. Last I knew my orders were to deliver a couple of engineers to help repair an energy station. What the hell is going on?"

"I don't know." Larik frowned and rubbed his jaw, apprehension crawling up his spine. Rapt One had a reputation as a peaceful colony as far as he'd been briefed, prosperous and powerful, and his assignment had sounded simple enough. "I suppose it could be standard but it does seem a bit excessive."

"Excessive?" Trey York handled the controls with effortless expertise, slowing the craft to comply with the signals flashing on the response screen. "See the glowing red? They've armed their weapons."

"It doesn't make any sense. They know who we are."

"Maybe the lieutenant knows something we don't."

"I think I'll go ask." Larik slid out of his seat and made his way toward the back of the small craft. He was puzzled by the show of aggression from a colony that had close ties to Minoa and requested him specifically to deal with a massive generator that according to the report provided power for millions of colonists. The governor had written the authorization himself. Apparently he feared the actual design was the trouble for the constant failures, and had asked the Council for an expert outside assessment.

The lieutenant sat in the galley at a small table, a cup at her elbow and her gaze fastened on a small reading device in her hand. She glanced up as he entered, her fine brows drawing together as she registered his expression. "Something wrong, Armada?"

As usual, even with apparently six hostile craft hovering with weapons pointed, he found it hard not to stare. She wore regulation dress uniform for their arrival, the fitted tunic and trousers showing off nice curves beneath the no nonsense style, and her glossy ebony hair pinned into a neat chignon. Eyes of deep violet framed with lush dark lashes stared at him in question from an oval face and her soft mouth—a delectable perfect pink color—parted under his intense regard.

He'd fantasized about her mouth lately, he had to admit. Actually, ever since he'd met the engineer the military assigned to assist him, he'd had an erection half the time, especially in the past two weeks since they'd left the main ship and been on the transport in such close quarters. It was damned uncomfortable and he would be glad when they didn't have to spend so much time together. She treated him with cool, professional indifference so it didn't seem like he ever would get to test out his fantasies firsthand and the frustration wasn't his idea of fun.

He jerked his attention back to the present. "Any idea why our welcome to Rapt One is a bit less than friendly? They're not letting us dock but taking us in themselves. To make sure we cooperate, they are making quite a statement."

Aspen Thorne looked puzzled and shook her head. "No briefing to any problem came through."

Even as she spoke the transport lurched and shuddered as the lock beam caught it. It was a little eerie to hear the pilot kill the thrusters so the small craft could be drawn in. The lieutenant swore and grabbed her cup as it slid to the edge of the table, narrowly missing getting the contents in her lap. "I guess you aren't kidding about the lock beam. I wonder what's up."

His cock, Larik thought in cynical amusement, but some of it wasn't just the gorgeous lieutenant but also the journey from Minoa. Abstinence had some drawbacks and he was more than ready to land on Rapt One and find a willing female. All planets with military based colonies had a ready supply and he needed one.

"I suppose we'll find out soon enough," he commented as she rose. "I think we'd better go prepare to dock. We're supposed to meet with the governor as soon as we disembark."

She nodded and followed him back toward the passenger seats, strapping in next to him. Moments later they were stationary, and before long the silent swoosh of the doors lifting signaled their arrival.

"Armada, Lieutenant Thorne, do you see what I do?" York stood at the door nearest the cockpit of the craft, his tall, lean body unnaturally rigid. He glanced back as they moved forward and his mouth quirked in a mirthless grin. "Our welcome seems less than enthusiastic."

Larik peered past him and also stiffened. Three figures stood waiting, their attire obviously full anti-contamination gear, from the huge helmets and breathing apparatus to the all-body suits. That was bizarre enough, but the loaded weapons pointed their way with unmistakable menace made him wonder just what hell might be going on.

One of them signaled for them to exit the transport. The dark-haired young pilot muttered, "I don't know about you two, but all that gear makes me wonder if it's a great idea to step outside. What do they not want to be exposed to that is fine for us?"

"I have no idea but they're the ones with the weapons and from what I've seen so far, they seem to mean business." Larik stepped past him and went down the ramp, slightly lifting his hands in a universal signal of surrender. Lieutenant Thorne went next, and Trey York followed along. Their three escorts led them through the first lift gate and down a long hallway through a door. Each were handed a bundle and pointed in the direction of a series of what looked like small cubicles.

"They want us to change our clothes?" Aspen Thorne didn't look too enthusiastic about the lightweight garments, a simple pullover shirt and loose fitting pants. "I'm beginning to really want an explanation over all of this."

"I'm going to guess by the stance of our not so friendly and not at all talkative guards here, they aren't going to give it." Larik eyed one of the figures, the man's face obscured by not just the helmet but the breathing mask over his mouth and nose. "I can't really see we have a choice."

Inside the cubicle instructions printed on a small plaque on the wall stood out. Complying, Larik removed every item of clothing and then slipped on the simple shirt and pants, leaving everything, including his boots, in the bin provided.

Lieutenant Thorne emerged last, the tight set of her mouth showing her displeasure and he could see why at once. The shirt provided left very little to the imagination, the thin material molding to her full breasts and even giving a pretty good idea of the dusky color of her nipples.

As he suspected, the lady had very nice tits.

Under his breath, York said, "I always wanted a better look at her set, but this isn't quite how I imagined it. The guys with the face masks kind of take away from the moment."

Larik stifled a laugh.

One of the guards lifted his weapon, pointing it at her head. Both Larik and York stepped forward at once in involuntary protective protest and the other two escorts intercepted them. Shoved back, there was little they could do.

Lieutenant Thorne went a little pale but lifted her chin and stared at the threatening soldier. "What?"

"I think he wants you to take down your hair." Larik realized the unspoken request with a rush of relief. "Give him the clip. I don't think we're supposed to have anything we arrived with on us."

"Oh." She quickly slipped it free and handed it over. Shining dark hair tumbled over her shoulders and down her back and she looked very different at once, not the neat military engineer with a business-like manner and cool, aloof poise, but like a woman with tumbled tresses and that to die for body.

Only he really wasn't interested in dying, Larik decided, eyeing the arsenal around him.

Not in the least.

* * * *

A small suite of utilitarian rooms with a main area, several places to sit, and a functional galley awaited them. At the back, sleeping quarters with narrow bunks lined up the walls, enough to sleep six individuals, plus an extra larger bed in the corner. There was also a cleansing room, modern and sterile. The impersonal feel of it wasn't exactly heartening and Aspen Thorne wondered how long they would have to wait around before someone bothered to explain their less than auspicious introduction to Rapt One.

Larik Armada dropped into a chair, his long legs carelessly extended, a frown on his face. Like all S-species males, he was very tall and gifted with an almost extraordinary handsomeness, his features symmetrical and masculine, his thick blond hair rumpled where he'd run his hand through it.. Vivid sapphire blue eyes reflected his emotions with startling clarity, including his sometimes less than reverent sense of humor. As a civilian he tended to take the military rules more as casual guidelines and his lax attitude toward protocol could be a bit of a problem now and then.

Which was exactly why she was included on this mission. Armada's brilliant intellect had no equal and there was nothing he couldn't do with the energy station all on his own. Aspen was along for the ride ostensibly to assist him, but mostly to make sure he followed procedure as much as possible.

If they ever got to the damn project. The ice cold reception wasn't exactly encouraging.

Trey York, the young pilot who'd been assigned to bring them over, paced restlessly over to the door, checked the scanning system for the second time, and shook his head. "We're fucking locked in." He registered his speech and glanced over. "Excuse me, Lieutenant."

"No problem." She agreed wholeheartedly with the sentiment, if not the choice of words. "I've heard it before. The question is *why* are we locked in?"

"They're worried we're carrying something, at a guess." Armada looked thoughtful, his lean body clad in the same generic tan pants and shirt, the nondescript color and fit doing nothing to lessen his almost overwhelming masculinity.

Actually, between the two of them, she felt overwhelmed in general. York was also a gorgeous S-species male, dark-haired and clean featured, with a whipcord athletic body and a vitality that was almost visible. She was twenty-five and she guessed the pilot might be her age or maybe a year or two younger and knew Armada wasn't yet thirty.

The space felt way too small to share with two males who exuded hormones and virility like most S-species. As a half-breed, she was stuck in a way between the Superhumans—or S-species—who dominated the known universe, and the humans from which they evolved, now considered inferior. Long ago genetic alterations—to make it easier for human beings to acclimate to different environments as Earth became too crowded and colonies were needed—resulted in a change that backfired for humans. Their counterparts grew more powerful, both physically and intellectually, and as a result, earth now existed under the thumb of the S-species in every way. Aspen's mother was a human female, and her father an S-species high-ranking soldier. Often, the breeding intermixed to make sure genetic mutations did not begin to occur and she was the result of one of those precautions.

York argued, "I've been through decontamination before after landing on more planets than I can remember. This is different."

"I agree." Aspen thought about sitting in the chair next to Armada, decided it was too close to both of them, and chose to lean against the wall. "Whatever has happened, they are keeping it low profile."

As if in answer, one of several screens on the wall flickered to life. "Very astute, Lieutenant Thorne. Low profile is correct. May I welcome all of you to Rapt One."

The image of the colony governor appeared. Though she'd seen his picture before, Aspen recognized the difference. Normally he was presented as an affable, good-looking administrator, a former admiral now in control of a prosperous colony, precise, agreeable, and competent. With dismay she registered the obvious signs of strain in the lines around his mouth and the weariness in his expression.

As liaison it was her job to respond, so she said neutrally, "Good afternoon, Governor. Forgive our speculation, but I doubt you can blame us."

It looked like he was seated in some sort of conference room and someone spoke off camera. He nodded and glanced at a small screen to his left and then back up. "I'm sorry for the inconvenience but please understand it is necessary. A recent biological attack on the colony could have killed thousands, maybe even everyone. We're doing our best at damage control at this point, and that means prevention."

Well, that explained the confiscation of their clothing and personal items at least. She frowned. "Has Minoa responded?"

"I've spoken to Governor Kartel, naturally. All the colonies are going on full military alert. He is as harried and concerned as I am, maybe more, since he sits on the Universal Council. He sends his greetings, Armada."

Aspen hadn't realized Larik was such close friends with one of the most powerful men in interstellar politics. She interjected, "Have there been other incidents?"

"It was the consensus after the first near disaster we would keep our precautions quiet for as long as possible. We'd like to be able to discern who is behind the terrorism so we can retaliate and eliminate the threat. Obviously word will spread soon enough of the required quarantine when entering the colony, but until then, we hope to not only prevent another attack, but if other infected arrivals are detected, maybe we can pinpoint the source."

"I can assure you we are not contaminated."

"No, you can't, Lieutenant. The previous individuals had no idea. As much as we need help with the defunct power station from Mr. Armada and yourself, you will have to wait out the quarantine like everyone else. We can go on with rationing power as before, but I cannot ration life."

The finality in his tone made her straighten a little, but it was Trey York who asked in a terse voice, "How long?"

"Eight weeks."

He stared, and his eyes, a light crystalline blue, glittered. "Did you just say *eight weeks*, sir?"

"We're being very careful." The governor's voice held an implacable edge. "The quarters you now occupy will hold you until the end of specified allotment. You'll find sufficient food and anything else you might require for your stay. At any time, you can communicate with us, but I'm afraid should any of you fall ill, no medical assistance will be given. The first physical contact you'll have will be the day you are released."

Sixty days? Aspen felt dismay roll over her like a wave and she saw the two men in the room exchange a swift glance, as if an unspoken communication passed between them. Armada spoke up. "May I request, sir, that Lieutenant Thorne be moved to separate quarters." He added in a bland tone, "We were out for months prior to our arrival."

In other words, for an S-species male, with their high sex drive, that was a long time. She'd noticed in the two weeks on the transport their restlessness and careful avoidance of contact with her if possible. They were already on the edge. If things had gone as expected, she had no doubt both of them would have sought female company for the night.

The governor shook his head. "The other quarters are all occupied and all have males. Besides, if we were going to introduce a new individual, their quarantine would have to begin again. I'm sure you understand this is difficult for everyone. We are in an official state of emergency on Rapt One and technically, you three are prisoners of war until it is proven you are safe. I am sure Lieutenant Thorne remembers her military training when it comes to certain situations. The 051 regulations were put in place for a purpose, and I'm afraid this is just one of those instances."

Aspen stared at the screen. "Sir, I—"

He cut her off ruthlessly. "I look forward to welcoming you to Rapt One in person in two months."

The screen abruptly went blank. The resulting silence seemed heavy and Aspen could feel from the heat in her face and neck she was flushed. No one spoke for a moment until Armada elevated a dark blond brow in a graceful arch. "Okay, I'll ask. Since I'm non-military, I'm not familiar with regulation zero-whatever. Mind filling me in?"

Already York looked at her differently. She could almost feel the change in assessment from respectful subordinate to predatory male. He said with deceptive casualness, "Regulation 051 states that in case of prolonged close contact between female personnel with males who have no other alternative for sexual release, it is part of their duties to assist in the welfare of their counterparts by providing them access to sexual intercourse. Believe me, during initial training, every new male soldier memorizes that one."

"Yeah, I would guess he would." Armada's sapphire eyes darkened a little.

"I'm going to venture a guess that's what the extra bed in the bunkroom is for. The sleepers aren't big enough for more than one individual." York sounded nonchalant but there was nothing casual about the way he looked at her.

He was right, she realized. Most big ships had a similar set up. Practicality dictated to have a separate comfortable place provided for sexual purposes since the sleeping berths were narrow by necessity to save space.

It was time for her to say something and take charge of the situation, she just had no idea what it should be. Aspen cleared her throat. "The regulation is more for combat instances than something like this."

"It seems to me the governor just told us we were prisoners of war." York gave her a cheeky grin. It lit his already disturbingly handsome face and she felt her flush deepen.

"Watch it, Pilot." Her voice should have sounded crisp and heavy with authority. Instead it came off with a small wobble.

He didn't look impressed with the warning, propping himself with one broad shoulder against the opposite wall, that teasing smile lingering. "I've been watching, ma'am, since the moment I met you. I like what I see, too, if I have permission to say so. How about you, Armada?"

"Oh yeah." The agreement was said in a low sexy drawl. "But I have a feeling the lieutenant already knows that."

She'd known they were both aware of her as a female, but they had been deferent and polite since they'd left the ship together for Rapt One. As a military pilot, York wasn't exactly under her command and carried no rank but was instead classed by experience and ability, for pilots were a separate division entirely. The same thing could be said for Armada, since he was civilian.

The 051 regulation also clearly stated no female was ever required to sleep with a male if she outranked him. Unfortunately for her, the rule did not apply here. Besides, essentially the governor had given them permission to expect her cooperation.

Four months of abstinence is a stretch for any S-species male. It seemed she had two on her hands and there was never a time in her career, even through the rigorous training required to get to where she was and rise in rank, she had felt so intimidated.

Would it be best to confess the truth? It put her at a disadvantage, but she was there anyway.

With as much dignity as possible, she said, "I'm a virgin."

Chapter 2

What the fuck? Trey York blinked, not sure he'd heard correctly. Anyone that looked like Thorne had to be sexually experienced.

Except she had lost some of her usual icy reserve and the set of her mouth was vulnerable as she stood there. If she could find anywhere to run, she would, Trey guessed. Chin lifted, her striking violet eyes flashing challenge, she looked composed but her soft lips trembled just a fraction in betrayal of her uncertainty. The cascade of her glossy dark hair fell almost to her waist, which really aroused him. He couldn't wait to see her naked because she was exactly his type, slender but curvaceous, her beauty delicate and feminine. He doubted she was full S-species because she wasn't as tall as most females of their kind, which was another nice bonus if he was stuck in such close quarters for two damned months. Human females were small and tight and it added to the pleasure of taking them to bed. His cock started to stiffen just thinking about it.

Trey repeated like an idiot, "You've never had sex?"

"That's what a virgin is last I checked." Her tone was caustic and she lifted one arched ebony brow.

"Pretty hard to believe." Armada looked just as surprised. "Males must pursue you all the time, Lieutenant."

"It doesn't mean I have to say yes."

"Until now," Trey pointed out.

"I'm aware of the regulation, thank you." To his amusement she shot him a lethal look. "I also get I'm outnumbered and at a pretty severe disadvantage size-wise."

"No one is going to force you to comply, Lieutenant, so relax on that point. Neither York or myself are that kind of male. We've flown together before so I can say that with confidence about Trey." Armada walked toward the door into the galley and selected a bottle from one of the shelves. He examined the label and shrugged. "We might get a little hard to live with, but it's your choice. You've been an officer long enough I imagine you understand how long abstinence affects males."

How true. One of the drawbacks to the enhanced sex drive genetically engineered into their physiology was aggression if not satisfied on a regular basis. Many ships on long voyages carried human female slaves to service the males but the two month trip from Minoa considered just on the inside limit of endurance and none had been provided. Had the voyage been any longer, neither of them would be so on the edge because there would have been relief available on the ship.

The current situation was just plain damned inconvenient.

Two more months would start to take its toll. Two more months with a gorgeous female companion spelled pure torture if they couldn't touch her, especially someone as intriguing as Aspen Thorne. Manual release just wasn't enough, not with a beautiful woman around fueling their libido.

"I agree." Trey dropped into a chair so maybe his height wouldn't be so imposing and to hide his growing arousal. "The words force and sex don't fit together in my opinion. However, to make an argument for our side, I'd like to point out you don't know what you've been missing."

"And you are just the males to show me, I suppose." She folded her arms across her chest, the body language as unmistakable as the sarcastic observation.

"Let's just say I've never had any complaints." He gave her an irreverent wink.

"I'm sure you'd find my inexperience boring."

"I'm sure I wouldn't. I think you're very beautiful, Lieutenant, if a little on the icy side. Thawed out a bit, I'd bet you'd make one hot female in bed. As for experience, no worries. Just lie back and spread your legs. We'll take care of the rest."

Aspen Thorne didn't seem to know how to respond to his blunt suggestion. She'd been blushing since the governor mentioned the regulation and the color in her smooth cheeks deepened even more. "That's very romantic, Pilot."

"Are we talking about romance?" he asked mildly. "I thought we were talking about sex. It's not the same thing."

"I agree. Maybe that's why I haven't found a male yet I felt strongly enough about to share the experience."

So the lovely lady had a hidden sentimental streak under that practical cool exterior. Trey elevated his brows and got back to his feet, well aware of Larik watching in amusement as he poured a glass of wine from a tall, cool bottle. As Trey walked toward her, he registered the flare of panic in her eyes but Aspen stood her ground. He said softly, "I can be damned romantic, Lieutenant."

"Don't put yourself out, York."

"It's in a good cause, so no trouble, ma'am." He reached for her and felt the tension in her slender body as he slowly pulled her into his arms but she didn't resist. The soft feminine feel of her next to him sent his nerve-endings on full alert. His cock, already stiff and high, pulsed.

Hell yes, he was going to make her want it. He didn't care much about the regulation or her sense of obligation to follow the rules. The truth was, the minute he saw her he'd wanted her and his determination to fulfill that goal was pretty high now that it was actually within his reach.

He stared into her eyes and then let his lashes drift down as he lowered his head. She didn't fight it when he took her mouth, but neither did she participate when he kissed her with every bit of finesse learned from years of experience with a variety of different females.

At least she didn't participate *at first*. He stroked his tongue into her mouth and felt the first shiver of response with a sense of easy triumph, keeping the kiss tender and gentle. One of her hands came up to rest on his chest, palm flat, as if she would push him away, but she didn't. He splayed his fingers on the graceful curve at the base of her spine and nestled her against his rampant erection. He tangled the other hand in her silky hair.

The stiffening of her body told him she felt every hard inch of his erect cock. Briefly he broke the kiss, sliding his mouth along her cheek to whisper in her ear. "You have all the power here, Lieutenant. Feel my need?"

"It's a little hard to miss, Pilot." The reply was tart, but she didn't try and pull away.

"Hard is the operative word." He gave a muffled laugh and kissed her again, with the same care and patience, a slow dance of tongue to tongue, of exploration and persuasion.

When he lifted his head they were both out of breath and he thought he might ejaculate just from holding her close. He wondered if Armada was having fun watching, and glanced over. The engineer stood negligibly by the small counter in the galley, sipping a glass of wine, but his brilliant blue gaze was fastened on them and the bulge at his crotch showed a definite enthusiasm for Trey's efforts with their gorgeous roommate. They'd shared females before, so this wasn't a new game, though normally they were willing women, eager for sex, not a virginal military officer with an obvious reluctance to let go of that reserve she used like a shield.

"This is where you tell me to go sit back down. Otherwise, we take this to the next level." It took Trey a great deal of effort to make the offer and he didn't let her go, gazing down at her face.

"If I say no now, I still doubt my ability to keep you two at arm's length for eight weeks. Let's not forget you could report me for failure of duty." An edge of resignation colored her voice.

Was she looking for an excuse to give in? Trey had to wonder, feeling the erect tips of her breasts against his chest through the thin material of the garments provided. Her body responded, whether or not she liked the situation. He caressed the small of her back in a slow circle, keeping her loosely against him. In a way, he didn't blame her for feeling pushed into a corner because the minute the governor brought up 051, it was like being issued an order.

Still, if she said no, he'd back off. With the looming threat of two months of captivity staring him in the face however, he took her answer as an oblique yes. "Let's move into the berth then," he suggested, unable to keep the husky note out of his voice. "You're going to like this, Lieutenant. My word on it."

* * * *

Had she agreed?

She wasn't sure. Those tender kisses had thrown her completely off course. He *could* be romantic, damn him, at least in a physical sense. Who would ever think a cocky military flyer could summon up that type of finesse. She'd met dozens and would never have anticipated it.

"Look, Pilot—"

"Call me Trey." His mouth swooped down and took hers again in one of those devastatingly hot kisses.

This situation wasn't the one she expected when she got the set of orders to accompany and assist Armada on Rapt One. Aspen was all too aware of the bed with some measure of apprehension, but it was tempered by York's self-assurance and the persuasive way he kissed her. Larik Armada carried that same air of easy confidence and in the two weeks alone with them on the transport, she'd discovered she actually liked both males. They were intelligent, had a sense of humor, and before this, had been carefully respectful.

What happened next would change the dynamics of their acquaintance beyond a shadow of a doubt. She couldn't help but wonder how her father, with his strict sense of military discipline, would feel about her predicament. On the one hand, he would have every expectation she would fulfill her duties. On the other hand, he *was* her father and she somehow doubted he would enjoy the idea.

Well, he was back on Minoa, serving the government there, and she was here.

With effort, she leaned back, breathing erratically. Unfortunately, Trey knew exactly how he affected her from the faint, attractive smile on his talented mouth.

His hands caressed her waist. "Since you haven't done this before, let me start by telling you naked is better. Lift your arms."

The request, given in a low sexy tone, was accompanied by a tug that pulled the less than adequate shirt she wore upward. Aspen let York pull it over her head, trying to fight the embarrassment she felt over being both half-naked in front of them and that her breasts felt tight and full. Her nipples actually tingled.

Warm hands cupped her flesh, lifting, weighing. "Very nice, Lieutenant." Trey's gaze was heavy as he fondled her, rubbing her nipples with palms, cradling her breasts with reverent care. "These are some spectacular tits."

"I'm glad you approve." The sarcasm in her tone was offset by a breathless gasp as he rubbed a thumb over one taut crest. Sensation streaked down to center between her legs and she wasn't prepared for the pleasurable rush of moisture. His long fingers looked dark against her paler skin.

"I think she likes that." Larik Armada spoke in his usual amused drawl. He'd set aside his drink and she felt him move up behind her. Warm lips grazed her nape as he lifted her heavy hair and nuzzled the back of her neck. "Let's get the rest off."

By the stars, there were two of them, one of her, and they both dwarfed her in size. Feeling outnumbered and out of her depth, Aspen was a little weak in the knees. York pulled loose the drawstring tie on the lightweight pants provided and eased the material down past her hips. It pooled on the floor and her whole body felt flushed as they both stared at her.

"Oh, hell yes." Trey York raked her bared body with a scorching glance. His crystalline eyes glittered. "That's pretty much what I've been imagining."

"We both have, let's face it. Let's move to the bed." Armada lifted her with what seemed like effortless ease, carried her into the sleeping chamber, and deposited her on the cool linens of the bed provided for just what they wanted from her. He leaned over, one arm braced on either side of her body, and his mouth brushed hers, lifted and then settled back in a long, leisurely kiss. Vaguely she was aware Trey took off his clothes, but her whole world seemed to be the seductive pressure of Larik's mouth and the light, teasing sweep of his tongue.

At twenty-five, even if she hadn't been to bed with any of the dozens of men who tried to get her there, she'd been kissed often enough. Before now, she hadn't really thought much of the process. These two seemed have a special talent or a hell of a lot of practice. Maybe both. There was no doubt she was beginning to feel strangely unafraid of what was going to happen, a languid sense of enjoyment replacing her trepidation.

She felt pressure on her thighs, easing them apart. Trey's palms were gentle but insistent. "Spread open, Lieutenant. I promise you're really going to melt down over this. I've yet to meet a female who doesn't."

She was innocent physically, but not uneducated. Men and women pleasured each other orally, but she had no idea of the exact sensation. Larik continued to kiss her, exploring her mouth, and one of his long-fingered hands stroked her bared breast, playing with the erect nipple. But at her jerk of reaction over the first warm lick across her labia, he chuckled and broke away.

His sapphire eyes held both fire and the usual teasing glint. "I don't want to distract you. Just enjoy. If you've never climaxed, I'm glad I'm going to get to see your first time. Relax and let it happen."

Trey's dark head nestled between her open legs, his mouth grazing her pussy. Aspen wasn't sure if it shocked or aroused her. Both probably. His long fingers parted her folds and he made a low sound in his throat as he laved the sensitive exposed tissue.

She thought for a moment she would go through the ceiling as he found a spot that made sweat prickle out over her skin.

It felt…incredible.

"Now this is one sweet pink little clit." He opened her further and she could feel the coolness of the air on that vulnerable bundle of nerves. With a light exhale, he blew across it.

Aspen fought an undignified moan. When he began to tease her clitoris with the tip of his tongue, the sound escaped anyway. Pleasure washed over in warm waves, like the thermal heated seas of Minoa, lapping, enveloping, consuming.

She spread her legs wider and arched her back, panting as her whole body quivered. Trey continued the erotic assault, first licking until the room seemed to spin, and then moving downward to spear his tongue into her opening, invading her pussy with sexy, hot strokes before moving upward again to circle her clit.

Something incredible happened. She could feel it in her breasts, in the tense coil in her stomach, and in the pulsing need between her legs. Two strong hands cupped her ass and lifted her hips and he pressed his mouth fully against her and suckled.

Her world tore apart. The savage pleasure shot her into space and she shut her eyes at the power of it, her body shaking uncontrollably as something snapped and broke and she let out a primal, unrestrained scream of enjoyment. The contractions in her vagina rippled over and over and she fought for breath, the exquisite sensation so acute she could not believe it.

A few moments later, limp and disbelieving at her uninhibited reaction, she felt Trey kiss her inner thigh. There was just the slightest smug note to his tone when he said, "I promised you would like it, Lieutenant."

How mortifying to know that not only was he right, but she'd had quite an audience for her abandoned reaction to her climax. With reluctance, she lifted her lashes.

* * * *

Larik wasn't sure what was more arousing, the sight of one of the most beautiful females he'd ever seen sprawled on the bed, legs still apart, her slim thighs streaked with moisture from her sexual fluids, or the almost dazed look on her flushed face in the aftermath of her first orgasmic experience. Any doubts he had over her acquiescence to their needs were banished by what he had just seen of her passionate side. He'd suspected it existed all along.. Outwardly she might seem like a cool female, but obviously she guarded that facet under the guise of an aloof, business-like professional.

Yes, the military officer was part of her, but the woman was in there also, all wrapped up in one of the most delectable packages he'd ever seen.

Long supple limbs, alabaster flawless skin, and all that long raven hair, right now spilled over the pale bed in a glossy pool.

York was right, her breasts were spectacular, full, high and firm, the flesh quivering as she still fought for each convulsive breath, tipped by dusky rose nipples he couldn't wait to taste.

As if choreographed, he and Trey both climbed on the bed at the same time, one on each side. Larik reached out and touched her cheek, meeting her eyes, immersing himself in the unusual violet depths. "I want to be your first," he said in a low voice, hearing the huskiness he couldn't control with inner rueful amusement. "Trey gave you your first orgasm. Let me be the first male to mate with you."

He'd removed his clothing and she seemed to focus finally, her eyes widening as she took in the long length of his erect cock. "I'm half-human."

A chuckle came up from his chest, he couldn't help it. "I know. That'll make it even better for both of us. I'm sure you know that S-species males and human females enjoy each other in a unique way. Our larger size enhances it for you, and your tightness makes it even better for us."

"I don't like being submissive to S-species simply because I'm half-bred." She sat up, shaking back her tangled, gleaming hair.

That he'd already guessed. "No one expects you to be. I think you have a mistaken perception of sexual intercourse, Lieutenant. This is not something we *do* to you, but something we can enjoy together."

York caught her shoulders and eased her back down. "He's right. As you discover what you like, let us know. We'll be more than happy to oblige. If there is something you don't like, tell us that too. Not all females are the same by any means."

Larik eased over so he lay on top of her, guessing the most traditional position the best place to start. She didn't resist as he used his knees to push her legs apart, but he did catch the flash of understandable apprehension in her lovely face. For reassurance, and because he liked her silky taste, he kissed her again, the pressure of his mouth on hers slow and deliberate, his tongue sliding in and out in a mimicry of what was about to happen. He stroked her hip and then slipped his hand between her open thighs, exploring her wet pussy, her recent orgasm leaving her soft, pliant, and slick.

In other words, ready.

Praise the stars and the moons, for he was heavy and aching, his balls so full he worried he might ejaculate the minute he got inside her. When he brushed her swollen clit she made a low soft sound he found immensely sexy, especially since he knew she wished to keep control of her reaction.

With one finger, he penetrated her, and ascertained she spoke the truth if he couldn't tell already from her reaction to each touch, each kiss. The heated tightness of her passage still had her barrier, the membrane of her hymen unbroken.

He whispered against her lips, "I will be as gentle as I can, Aspen."

The use of her first name made her lashes drift up, but she didn't say anything as he positioned his cock and just rubbed the tip at her moist entrance. Beneath him she shifted a little, and took a deep breath.

"Relax your inner muscles," Larik instructed, his control a mere thread. "Make your body let me in and don't tighten against it. If you concentrate on staying open and accepting, there won't be much discomfort, even this first time."

She closed her eyes and nodded, a swallow rippling the muscles in her slender throat as the engorged tip of his cock pressed against the small opening into her vagina, stretching it until the swollen head of his penis slid in. Larik worked his cock slowly into her with tiny thrusts and withdrawals, doing his best to go slow, his muscles starting to shake as he fought for control, well aware of York watching them with a heavy-lidded gaze.

She was small, hot, and like satin inside, her walls holding him in a perfect erotic embrace. "Am I hurting you?" he managed the question between his teeth.

"No. Yes. I'm not sure." She lifted her hips a telltale fraction that told him what her body wanted, even if her mind hadn't firmly decided yet.

It was his pleasure to slide in the fraction more it took to break through. He impaled her with his entire length, going deep against her womb. The beautiful lieutenant did little other than give an inarticulate cry and her hands flew up to grasp his shoulders.

He brushed his mouth against her smooth cheek in reassurance. "That's it."

"I hope not, Armada, or else the whole thing is overrated."

The challenge in her voice made him give a low dark laugh. "I meant as far as it being uncomfortable. As for the rest, well, no problem, I'll be happy to show you."

He began to move, first a slow slide backward and then the hot-blooded surge forward, need running through his veins and prickling his nerve-endings. She was exquisitely tight, just as he'd imagined all too often since their introduction, and the erotic friction of their joining sent pulses of pleasure through his entire body.

By the third thrust Aspen had caught the rhythm with ease, her hips undulating to his movements, lifting to take him as deep as he could go, her beautiful eyes half-closed and her lips parted. Experienced enough with female arousal, he understood each nuance in the change in her breathing and soon small, almost inaudible pants turned into full-fledged uncontrolled moans.

Her small hands, resting on his shoulders, signaled her need, the nails lightly scoring his flesh.

Fuck, yeah, sweetheart. Mark me.

He could come at any moment. The restraint was for her.

"Faster?"

"Do something…oh…oh…" She gasped and he could feel her inner muscles start to tighten in a betraying clench as the first wave hit her. Now her nails drew blood.

It was like flipping a switch. One second he was in charge, holding off his orgasm, and then next her body took over and gave him no choice. As her spasms began to squeeze his surging cock, he lost it and the rush of his release so consuming lights flashed behind his eyes and it felt like a solar system had combusted.

He was fairly certain he had never ejaculated so fiercely in his life. Shuddering, shaking, he emptied into her for what felt like an eternity and found himself barely cognizant enough to keep from collapsing on top of her. Instead he fell to the side, pulling her with him. She also trembled, her breath warm against his neck as she sprawled across his chest.

York drawled in an amused, laconic voice, "Maybe two months doesn't seem that bad after all. Come here, Lieutenant."

"I couldn't possibly."

The words were mumbled against Larik's damp skin and he grinned, obligingly easing away and transferring her lax form to Trey's waiting arms. The lady might just surprise herself, he thought, her innate sexuality not a question in his mind. That luscious body represented not just a beautiful female, but a very responsive one.

"We'll take our time. No rush." York's long fingers drifted through her gleaming dark hair. "I don't mind just touching you until you're ready."

The soft words at odds with his rigid cock, Larik appreciated they were both on the same plane when it came to Aspen. Sexual pleasure was about sharing, not taking. It was good they both thought the same way. If he had to be trapped in close quarters with another male for so long, he was glad it was Trey. Not only was he a talented pilot, but since they'd flown together several times before, they were also good friends. Sharing a female without acrimony wasn't always easy for a male, and it helped to like your partner.

Besides, watching was almost as good as doing. Not quite, but close.

His whole body still humming, he watched through half open eyes as Trey coaxed her with soft words and light kisses, playing with her beautiful breasts, sucking her nipples to rosy-tipped high points, stroking her inner thigh but not stimulating her clit, even when it started to become clear she was aroused again.

"Show me what you want, Lieutenant." He licked the side of one pale, perfect breast in a wicked sweep of his tongue, his grin impudent. The silk of his dark hair brushed her skin, a superimposition of ebony and alabaster white.

"I ...thought...you were the one in such a hurry to get me here, Pilot." Her response was thready and there was a hint of accusation in those magnificent violet eyes. She took in a shuddering breath as his fingertips just grazed her wet pussy, teasing her.

"Call me Trey, remember? And for the record, I never hurry sex. I could play all day with a body like yours, so you're just going to have to let me know when you want it." Tall and dark, his body corded with muscle, he was a stark contrast to her delicate femininity.

Larik stifled a chuckle at the lift of Aspen's chin in stubborn refusal. If the stinging on his shoulders was any indication, the lady had enjoyed what just happened between them as much as he had, and that was saying a lot. Whatever her mind wanted, he had a feeling that very hot, sexy body was going to betray her.

A few more calculated caresses later she spread her legs, catching York's shoulders and urging him on top of her. The young pilot complied with alacrity, the bunched muscles in his shoulders indicating his self-control wasn't effortless. With impressive slow care, he pushed his rigid cock into her pussy until he was finally buried to his balls, his face reflecting his pleasure.

"Jesus, that's good. Tight and hot."

"Move, Pilot."

"Trey."

"Fine, Trey." She shifted beneath him, all restless panting need.

"Yes, ma'am."

He began to move in long slow thrusts, male into female, and from the sheen of sweat on his forehead the discipline came with a price. Under him, Aspen arched and moaned and Larik marveled at her awakening sexuality and incredible beauty.

The instinct to mate, old as time itself, was a driving animalistic force but also a miracle, he decided as he saw the first wild quiver when she went over the edge. Trey gave an answering groan, his tall body going rigid, his eyes tightly shut and his buttocks flexing as they climaxed together.

Two months wasn't really that long after all, Larik decided with a languid sense of contentment. Not with the exceptional Lieutenant Thorne for company.

Chapter 3

Ran Kartel stared out the window of his office, seeing the spectacular view of the First City without taking it in, his mind occupied with other thoughts, the least pleasant the idea of a war with an unknown adversary.

"Governor?" The undersecretary hovered in the doorway, obviously not sure how to handle the situation.

Ran turned. "Go ahead and show him in."

"At once, sir."

His visitor was an acquaintance, no more, but how could he refuse to see someone so high-ranking with such a distinguished service record. Since he had a very busy day, not to mention council meetings over the Rapt One incident, his schedule did not make it easy to see anyone who didn't have an appointment but Ran had an idea why General Thorne had decided to pay him an impromptu visit.

The general was a tall man, his dark hair just showing threads of silver, his clear-eyed gaze and bearing an indication of why he'd achieved such a high rank. He came in and nodded briskly. "Good morning, Governor. I appreciate you seeing me."

"No problem, General. What can I do for you?"

"How bad is it?"

Short and to the point. Well, he didn't really blame the man. "I assume we are talking about Rapt One. Please, sit down. I'll tell you what I can."

"I'm cleared on the highest security levels, sir." Thorne chose a chair and sank into it, his gaze direct.

Ran had the ability to tell what other people were thinking with uncanny precision and he could feel the other's man's tension, his worry, and underneath it all, a sense of outrage under the calm façade.

He didn't really blame him.

"I know your clearance, General. Rest assured, I'll tell you what I know, but it really isn't much. I received a communiqué recently that there was what we think might have been terrorist activity directed at the Rapt One colony. I've spoken with the governor there and he feels the problem is contained, but we are at a loss as to who might have been behind it. As you know, it's one of the outermost planets, so we monitor security there at the highest level."

"I hope so. I understand my daughter is there. I am not happy about that on several levels at this moment. I came to request she be recalled."

Ran had a feeling that was what this visit was about. Unfortunately, even though he understood the general's point of view clearly enough—he had a daughter himself—his hands were tied on the matter. "The quarantine is a necessary step, wouldn't you agree? Until we figure out how and why the first contaminated individuals became infected, we can't trust the fate of thousands of citizens on the hope no one else has been exposed."

"She's an officer with a spotless record of service."

"Yes, she is I understand. Congratulations, you must be quite proud of her. But," Ran paused, searching for the right thing to say, because he truly was sympathetic, before continuing quietly, "but it does not make her exempt from possible contamination. The virus could have come from anywhere. It's been substantiated it's synthetically engineered, it's fatal, and no risks are being taken."

"I could pull York's personnel file but know nothing about Armada, except his reputation as a talented engineer. He isn't a solider." The general stated the words without inflection but the unspoken question was there.

Well, Ran supposed if his daughter was trapped on a distant planet locked in with two S-species males, he'd also be damned concerned about her welfare. "I know nothing about the pilot myself, but I can tell you Armada is not only brilliant intellectually but he will treat your daughter well."

"You sound sure."

"I know it to be a fact," Ran said bluntly. "I traveled with Armada on a diplomatic mission and we became good friends. I trust him."

Thorne sighed. "She's half-human," he admitted, and added on a murmur, "and very beautiful."

Not something either male would likely overlook, not for that length of time.

Sometimes it was hell to be a father, Ran thought with silent sympathy.

* * * *

The warm water ran in streams over her skin and Aspen tilted her head back, wetting her long hair, one hand braced on the wall of the washing cubicle. The dried residue on her thighs was sticky and she rinsed it off, amazed at the prodigious amount of sperm produced by S-species males.

Doing her duty hadn't been quite as much of a sacrifice as she thought. To her chagrin, it had turned out to be disturbingly wonderful.

All her life she'd been taught the merits of order and control. There had been very little control in the way she'd responded to first Larik's lovemaking, and then succumbed to the impudent Flevel pilot, no doubt fueling his already formidable confidence. By the stars he'd even tasted her pussy and she was pretty sure there wasn't an inch of her he hadn't touched.

They'd promised she would enjoy it and she had. Both males knew it.

Surely there were worse things in the universe than having two wildly attractive, considerate lovers, wasn't there? Of course there were, she told herself with prosaic meditation, but the trouble was she had always imagined her sexual life would be in tune with her emotional one. Maybe it was her human side, but Trey was right, she did have a romantic ideal over what she wanted when it came to choosing a mate. Physical desire was important, of course, but she liked the notion of love. Her father had mated with her mother for strict procreation purposes and after her birth, they had gone their separate ways. Like most half-breeds, she had been given to her father to raise because humans were considered inferior and given very few rights. He had graciously allowed her to actually journey to earth and meet her birth mother, but she knew many half-bred children not given that opportunity.

In her opinion, both Larik Armada and Trey York typified their dominant race. They were highly intelligent, confident, virile males. Apparently they were *her* males for the next eight weeks.

Or rather, she thought with wry resignation, she was theirs. They had each mated twice with her the night before and she had the feeling that however inexperienced she'd been before their arrival on Rapt One, by the time the quarantine was over, she would have made up for lost time.

She finished bathing and stepped out, drying off and following the instructions on the plaque on the wall, much like in the cubicles where they'd changed their clothes. Nothing would be brought in so they had to be careful so they would have clean linens and clothing the entire duration of their captivity. The same thing with food and drink. There was plenty as long as they didn't waste any or overindulge.

She slipped into the regulation issue generic pants and shirt, brushed out her damp hair, and left the cubicle for the main area of their sparse quarters. There she found York in the galley, and Armada at one of the screens, a slight frown on his face as he stared at what looked like a computer model of the inside of a building. He glanced up as she came into the room. "Good morning, Lieutenant."

By the stars, she blushed like an idiot. "Good morning," she said briskly, trying to ignore the warmth in her face.

"Hungry?" Trey rummaged in the cooling unit and took out a package. He set it on a shining metal ledge flanked by chairs supposed to serve as the eating area and gave her one his devastating smiles, a hint of cocky male in the lift of one brow.

She was hungry, actually. Aspen inclined her head, hoping she looked cool and calm. "Thank you, yes." The dignified effect was spoiled when she went to sit down and winced.

"Sore?" he asked bluntly, unwrapping the food and setting it on a serving disk.

An embarrassing question but he was right, she was a little tender. No wonder, since they'd both been, well, *extremely* enthusiastic over the 051 regulation. "A little," she admitted as she accepted the food. When he handed her the disk, their fingers brushed and she couldn't believe the answering shiver that went through her body.

Trey York had very talented hands and it wasn't confined to the controls of a transport craft.

He looked thoughtful. "I'm going to bet there are lubrication capsules in the med kit. I'll look."

"I'll be fine," she said hastily, wanting to change the subject.

"Oh, Lieutenant, you are more than fine, let me tell you." He winked, the look in his crystal blue eyes telling her he found her morning after embarrassment amusing. "Your enthusiasm for doing your duty has made the next weeks trapped here sound like a vacation in paradise instead of a prison sentence."

"Is sex all you think about, Pilot?"

"That and flying," he admitted, unrepentant and teasing. "Two of my favorite things."

Not a surprising answer. He was as good as lover as he was a pilot. Still, Aspen wanted some measure of control over the situation. The night before, she hadn't had any. They'd taken over everything, her body, her senses, her will…

"Aspen, when you're done eating come look at this. Tell me I'm not wrong here."

The familiar use of her first name without her permission made her stiffen, but then again, she supposed considering she'd been intimate with him in the most basic of ways a female could be with a male, maybe Armada felt entitled. She didn't wait but got up and carried her plate over and stood behind him where he sat by the screen, staring at the model. "What am I supposed to be looking at?"

"I accessed the colony database. Here's our energy station. This isn't the same—"

She interrupted, "You did *what*?"

Larik looked up at her, his sapphire eyes glimmering. "Broke in. Hacked. Bypassed their defensive walls, whatever you want to call it."

She swallowed because her mouth had been half-full and she stared at him. "That's impossible."

"I was bored. It took me about two seconds. Anyway—"

"Armada, have lost your mind? It's a capital offense."

He shrugged his broad shoulders. "I used the governor's link. Right now the system thinks I'm him."

She wasn't sure whether to be impressed or horrified. That Larik Armada was a genius wasn't a surprise, but this recklessness was just why she had been sent along, she guessed. It was supposed to be her job to make him stick to regulations and impersonating the governor of a prestigious colony was definitely not on the agenda. Besides, it really was punishable by some not very desirable consequences and she found she didn't want anything like that to happen to Larik.

Shit. She could also get into trouble for this.

"Sign out," she ordered tersely. "Get off there before they trace this breach back to us. Here."

"They won't." He disregarded the order and pointed. "Stop worrying and look at this."

York had seated himself at the ledge. He said with a laugh, "If he says they can't trace it, Lieutenant, they can't. Trust me on that one. I think his brain is a machine."

That neither of them was worried didn't surprise her, for that same self-confident bravado seemed to seep from their very pores. In resignation, she leaned forward and focused on the image Armada wanted her to see.

It was the same energy station they'd been called in to assess, and at first glance all seemed to be in order. The blueprint she'd been sent to look at prior to their departure had a conventional design and gave no reason for the constant failure she could see, hence the trip to actually look at it firsthand.

"That's the station," she said slowly. "I've seen the design before. It shouldn't fail, but then again, there could be a defective part, a flawed transom—"

"Or," Armada said without inflection, "there could be some reason there's an extra circuit in the main control panel. It isn't in the original plans at all."

Until he pointed at it, Aspen would never have seen it. She furrowed her brows. It existed. A tiny innocuous line in the center of the screen. *No one* would notice it by glancing over the plans.

No one but Armada.

This was puzzling, no doubt about it. "What makes you think it doesn't have a purpose? Sometimes things are changed or added by the design engineers, you know that."

"Oh, I think it does have a purpose. It kills the power to entire thing."

"In one switch?" she objected, shaking her head, her food forgotten. "There's no way. The system has a dozen safeguards."

"Sure it does." He tapped a few buttons, and a new screen came up, an entirely different angle of the same plans. "All of those safeguards are shut down by this one small switch."

"You can't know that."

"I can know it. I *do* know it." Larik rubbed his jaw, narrowing those remarkable eyes. "The question is why? It isn't included in the plans originally sent to us. Why does someone continually shut down the power? Why would they want to?"

Aspen looked at the screen, her mind processing the information as a feeling of unease settled in her stomach. Her hunger deserted her all at once. "You think the failures are on purpose?"

"I think that someone put in a way to constantly shut off the entire grid when it is absolutely against all regulations and that means two things." His handsome face was set. "At the very least the chief engineer is involved and the governor has no clue what's going on or he wouldn't have sent for me."

York said coolly, "Because you spotted it at a glance. It kind of makes me wonder if we aren't stuck here to keep you from seeing anything else."

The same thought had already occurred to her. Unfortunately. She looked at York. "You honestly think there would be a plot to infect an entire colony with some rare disease in an effort to keep one man from spotting a single, almost invisible circuit in a harmless energy station?"

"I think it's possible." Trey crossed his arms over his broad chest. "What if the contamination is a diversion? Notice how the governor said thousands *could* have died. As far as we know, no one really did."

"Except the infected ones that brought in the disease, I'd guess, otherwise there wouldn't be such a panic." Aspen wandered back into the galley and deposited her plate, thinking furiously. She turned around. "We're just guessing. A bunch of what-ifs."

"We could talk to the governor."

No, they couldn't. The minute they did Governor Halden would know they slipped into the colony system or they couldn't have the information. "That would be quite a risk," she pointed out, trying to be the voice of reason. "We need to see the actual station, test your theory about the extra circuit. You think we're imprisoned now? The real thing would not include decent beds and food rations."

Larik leaned back, raking his hand through his hair.

Damn, it was distracting. She still remembered how it felt to run her fingers through those soft strands as he moved over her and in her. Deep in her as she sighed in pleasure...

And why the hell was she even thinking about that? The last thing the two of them needed was encouragement.

A light flashed and they all three glanced up.

"Time to get our daily check up," York said sardonically. "I've got to say I hope no one deliberately infected me to kill off genius boy here."

* * * *

The box was claustrophobic and he'd always had a problem with close spaces. Trey stepped in, let the laser run down his body as he held his breath, registering the screen readouts. Normal temperature, vital statistics all in line, and he stepped out. He'd been essentially kidding about his worry over being infected, but then again, what the hell might be going on?

Armada went next, standing in the small space built into the wall, his face impassive as the scan ran in less than a minute. He also left the cubicle quickly, and the beautiful lieutenant took his place.

They really *were* prisoners, Trey thought in grim realization. Not able to leave, having their bodies monitored, forced to eat rations, wear the clothes selected by their captors...it was more than a little disconcerting.

Of course, Aspen Thorne was the one consolation of the whole entire thing. He always enjoyed females, but she was different somehow. He wasn't sure why he felt that way, but he'd been drawn in the first time he saw her, and now that he'd had her, he was hungry for more. She had an intriguing mix of poise and intelligence, coupled with an undeniable sensuality that sent him past the stars. All regulations aside, he'd have done whatever it took to get her into bed.

She liked romance. Soft, sweet persuasive kisses, tender touches...

She'd liked sex, too. Even innocent she'd been responsive, and he couldn't wait until the next time he had her beneath him, his cock buried deep.

Or her on top of him. That idea had merit.

Well, hell, he hardened just thinking about it and the uniform issued by their Rapt One captors didn't hide much. Trey reached down and adjusted his stiffening cock as casually as possible and watched her and Armada head right back to the screen.

Engineers, he thought with an amused inner sigh.

"I probably shouldn't stay on too long," Armada finally admitted, his nimble fingers flashing across the board panel in front of him. "They can't trace it back here, but if there is something going on with the station, they might have safeguards in place to tell them if someone spends too much time looking over the site."

Aspen looked relieved, but a frown still creased her smooth brow. "I still can't see the point of it."

The screen went blank but Larik still stared at it for a moment, his sapphire eyes unblinking. Then he glanced up and smiled ruefully. "Neither can I, for now."

Then she did it. She licked her lower lip in an absent thoughtful mannerism as she pondered the discussion at hand, but Trey really could not help the rush of blood to his crotch.

Great, now he had a full blown erection.

It was the close quarters, he excused himself. A gorgeous available female and a very small space, nothing to do but think about how luscious her breasts looked under the thin shirt she wore, eight weeks of inactivity looming ahead. Since the day he'd been certified he hadn't gone that long without flying and he really needed a distraction from thinking about *that* aspect of their stay. To him being a pilot was like breathing and being grounded against his will rankled.

"Lieutenant?"

Aspen turned and her remarkable violet eyes widened as she took in him lounging against the doorjamb into their sleeping quarters, trying to look nonchalant but with a considerable bulge in his pants.

There wasn't much question what he wanted.

To his relief, she didn't look anything but a little surprised. Maybe even...pleased? It was hard to read her expression, but she didn't seem resistant to the idea, and that was all he cared about. Her ebony brows lifted. "Yes?"

"I'd really love to make this go away." He gestured at the stiff ridge clearly visible through the thin material between his legs, aware of Armada's chuckle. "You're too close," he explained briefly, his arousal throbbing even harder. "Too female, too tempting, too beautiful."

"How can any woman be too female?" she asked dryly, but actually took a step forward.

"You somehow manage," he told her. From the first moment he'd met her, the only thing he could think about was the fact she was a female and he was a male. It wasn't just her striking beauty, because he'd known plenty of gorgeous females in his lifetime and never been so drawn.

Never. It gave him pause.

However, his raging hard-on was in control at the moment so he'd just have to ponder that later.

"I just took a shower," she murmured as she walked toward him.

"Take another. You have a busy day planned?" He couldn't keep the slight sarcastic edge from the question.

"Very funny, Pilot."

Another step. Two more and she'd be close enough to touch. Trey realized with a start she *wanted* it. Wanted him. He knew enough about females to recognize that heavy look in a woman's eyes. Though he knew she'd very much enjoyed the night before, he was still a little astonished he didn't have to work harder to get her back in bed.

Who was he to argue with such easy success?

She stopped in front of him, her lacy lashes drifting downward, obviously expectant. Underneath the thin shirt her nipples stood already erect and prominent, leaving sharp points under the fabric.

Slow, he reminded himself with a swift intake of breath. She'd admitted to being a little tender from the night before. Trey reached out and ran his hands lightly down her arms as he bent his head to kiss her and she immediately leaned in to him, her body pressed suggestively against his erection.

And she moaned into his mouth.

It was a small sound but his already throbbing cock didn't really need more encouragement. In a flash he lifted her in his arms and took her into the sleeping area, depositing her on the bed. Dark silken hair spilled everywhere and the gorgeous lieutenant eagerly tugged off her shirt as he fumbled to get off her pants, his hands lacking their usual dexterity in his haste.

It did not help a bit when she said in breathless command, "Hurry."

Yes, ma'am.

He jerked off his own clothing in record time. One thing he could say for the garments provided by the Rapt One military for their quarantine prisoners, they were easy to get on and off. The pants slid down and he stepped free, his erection high and pulsing with the racing beat of his heart. Definitely one of his fantasies, he acknowledged silently, as he forced himself to stop and take a deep breath. Aspen Thorne lusciously naked, that needy look in her lovely violet eyes as she spread those long, gorgeous legs for him...

Which is exactly what happened. As he stood by the side of the bed, fighting for control so he could have at a modicum of finesse, she gazed up at him and opened her thighs. She was wet, damn wet, the lips of her labia glistening in carnal invitation.

He didn't need to be asked twice.

To hell with finesse, she wanted to be fucked. Fine, perfect, because he wanted to fuck her. The night before he'd thought of as more gentle initiation, but that didn't appear to be how she wanted it now.

He lowered his body on top of her supplicant one, positioning himself between her pale thighs. The head of his eager cock rubbed her slick folds and found her small opening. So small. Their disparate size came slamming home and he paused. "I don't want to hurt you," he managed to say in a voice that barely even sounded like his.

"I don't care...I don't think you will...just please, Trey." Full breasts quivered with her uneven breathing and her hands went to the small of his back.

"Tell me if I need to stop." He sure as hell hoped he could after making that outlandish offer.

Entering her was like being led through the gates of paradise, that is if paradise was hot, wet, and sublimely tight. He managed—a miracle because of the frantic push of her hands—to work in slowly, bit by excruciatingly wonderful bit, making her body accept his thick length until he finally fully sheathed his entire cock. He could feel the softness of her cervix against the tip of his shaft and see the flutter of her pulse in the slender column of her neck as he lowered his mouth to nuzzle just under her ear. "Okay?"

"Yes." The throaty quality of her response was matched by the slight arch of her back so he sank in a fraction more and she quivered. "Oh...oh."

He began to move, slowly at first, in measured withdrawal and cautious penetration, but it was obvious enough from her reaction she wanted it faster, more intense, and he was an obliging lover. As restrained as she normally appeared, she certainly wasn't at the moment he thought with male satisfaction. Lieutenant Thorne was all tumbled ebony hair, the flush of rising orgasmic pleasure on her skin, those striking eyes closed, her soft lips parted as she panted and met each of his thrusts with the lift of her pelvis.

Though he could normally put off climax until his partner achieved it, Trey wasn't at all sure that it would happen this time. Her unexpected eagerness aroused him above the normal level, and the pleasure of being inside her gripped him with unusual fierceness. A bead of sweat trailed down his jaw and he clenched his teeth, trying to hold on long enough for her to come.

It happened fairly swiftly considering how new she was to the game. Aspen began to shudder, those exquisitely responsive inner muscles starting to milk his plunging cock, and he lost it in a feverish response, a low groan erupting from his throat as he pumped sperm into her vaginal passage in a hot, fierce rush.

Panting and entwined, they both lay silent in the aftermath, but he stayed where he was, buried deep, his sated body humming in contentment. just holding her slender form in his arms.

It was a little jarring when she finally did speak, her face slightly averted. "What just happened?"

Trey rose up on one elbow, peering at her profile. She was embarrassed, he could see it even with the flush of post-orgasmic blood still under her smooth skin. Her cheeks were scarlet. "What do you mean?" he asked cautiously. Females occasionally had the most unusual reactions to certain situations and it seemed like she'd just asked one of those dangerous questions no male should venture to answer.

"I can't believe I acted that way."

Should he comment? Probably not, but the situation seemed to demand it. "Are we talking about the fact you apparently like sex? I, for one, think that's about the best news I've ever heard in my life."

* * * *

Aspen stared at the male S-species still cradling her in an intimate embrace, his all-too handsome face holding a faint expression of amusement, no doubt over how easily she'd been persuaded to fall right back into bed with him.

Hell, she realized in consternation, she hadn't even needed persuasion. It seemed like when she turned around and noticed his arousal, a switch flipped somewhere in her. That long cock was even now still in her, deliciously stretching her vaginal passage.

It felt...well, good, she had to acknowledge. The night before had been more than a little educational but it appeared that now that her body understood the pleasure of sexual interaction, it wasn't interested in her dignity in the least.

"I am not one of those females who bed every man they meet," she said stiffly.

"I know." To his credit, York didn't laugh at her. "I was there for your first time, remember?"

She did remember. He'd been the first male to touch her intimately and he'd audaciously used his mouth.

How many females had looked into those crystalline blue eyes and felt him hold them in the way he held her now? It went against every promise she'd ever made to herself to not have sexual relations with any male, much less a slightly arrogant—if undeniably attractive—military pilot, unless a deeper feeling was involved than simple physical attraction. "I think you should let me go."

"Why? I like it like this. Trust me, I'll be hard again in a minute." One eyelid dropped in an impudent wink. "We could stay here all day. What else is there to do?"

God, he had fabulous eyelashes. Thick and dark to match that tousled black hair and he felt so solid, all honed muscle.

Her pussy throbbed, filled and possessed by his girth. She'd always heard how gratified human females were by S-species men. Apparently her half-blood heritage betrayed her.

"I am not staying all day in bed," she declared and attempted to pull away.

Strong arms tightened just enough to keep her firmly in place, which was currently right up against his hard body. His gaze fastened on her mouth. "I barely kissed you the first time. Can I make up for that? You have most delicious mouth, Lieutenant, so soft and warm. Let's not forget I didn't even touch those gorgeous tits and I'm going to guess they feel neglected."

What was wrong with her? One tender, slow kiss later as his hands played over her breasts and she experienced that same rush of need. She could feel how wet she was as he began to move again, the glorious rush as he withdrew and sank his hard cock back into her yielding body, saturated with his semen, panting and willing beneath him.

She actually was little tender from the night before, but the discomfort was overridden by this out of control need.

And it really was apparently. Out of control. She slid her fingers through the softness of his hair, such a contrast to the corded hardness of his neck, kissed him back with unrestrained fervor, and climaxed twice before he finally shuddered and spilled against her womb in a hot, frenzied rush.

Maybe she *could* stay in bed all day, she thought in languorous contentment afterwards, damp and sated, a little stunned at her uncharacteristic behavior but not enough to keep her from drifting off to sleep.

Chapter 4

Ran stared at the message, thinking through his options. He hadn't been surprised necessarily to get a communication from the governor of Rapt One. Right now everyone who knew about the attempted biological attack watched the planet, not to mention their own point of entry ports, but despite the official insignia, the words had not been written by Halden.

Larik Armada was the author, no doubt about it. He'd made it cryptic enough if one of the undersecretaries had stumbled across it they wouldn't know what it meant, but Ran knew Larik and the way he worked. Of course, there was a disadvantage to being that brilliant. Sometimes you don't realize everyone doesn't operate on your level.

Rubbing his fingers at his temples, Ran read it again, trying to make sense of it.

De te fabula

Only in this case, me. More as things progress. Help would be appreciated in the cause of liberation.

The first part was in a language he knew had been dead even on earth for so long he barely remembered what it was called, but a flash of inspiration hit him and he swiftly pressed a button.

The familiar voice never failed to make him smile, even now, even with possible terrorists trying to infect entire colonies. "Hello, love."

"Hello, Governor." His wife's tone held a teasing note. "To what do I owe this honor in the middle of the day?"

"I need your help." He hadn't told her about the attack. He hadn't wanted to panic her over the possibility of a similar threat to Minoa, not so soon after she'd given birth to their second child.

"Of course." She sounded puzzled.

"What do you know of the old earth Latin?"

"The language? I suppose some. There are phrases that survived and became part of everyday speech."

He repeated the beginning of the message.

"I have no idea just like that, Ran. Why don't you have one of your assistants research for you?"

"Because if I did, I might clue them in that Larik has gotten illegally into the communications systems and is sending out messages under the guise of an important official." Leave it to Armada to infiltrate any type of device, any blocked structure as if all the technology poured into security was worthless.

"Oh." That single word spelled out her understanding of the seriousness of the situation. "May I ask why he would risk doing such a thing?"

"You may ask, but I wish you wouldn't."

"I hate it when you are cryptic. It usually means something is wrong."

Well, she might be exactly right. Only Armada would actually know an archaic phrase from a dead language on a distant planet and use it to try to get some oblique point across. "You're constantly reading earth books, Jerra. Can you try and see if you can figure it out for me?"

"You know I will."

"Thanks. I'll be home late."

"Darling, you always are."

He ended the communication with a small sigh. She was right about that too. Minoa demanded a lot of his time.

Help would be appreciated in the cause of liberation.

That part wasn't hard to understand. Armada wanted out of quarantine. As governor of the most powerful of the colonies, Ran wasn't sure he could manage that, even for an old friend. He wasn't sure he *should* manage it.

Well hell, he thought morosely and began a scan for the file again on the Rapt One incident that had the colony in current lock down. Maybe looking over the report would help him figure out what to do.

* * * *

The faint frown between his opponent's arched brows was a little amusing, and Larik had a feeling it would turn into a full-fledged scowl the minute she realized she was about to lose.

One slender hand hovered, descended, and she made her move.

He countered with lethal swiftness and the game ended in a victory.

Violet eyes sent him an accusing glare. "How do you do that?"

He gave Aspen an ingenuous look. "Do what?"

"She means you don't even have to think about it," Trey said, coming over to sit down at the small table, lounging in the chair with careless grace. "It's irritating as hell."

Larik grinned. "Sorry."

"Yeah, I can tell." Aspen sighed and waved her hand over the sensor, the game board disappearing from the surface in front of them all. "We've been here two weeks and I haven't won once."

"Let me make it up to you." He was honestly surprised he did win every time because she was so damned distracting. Something was going on because he couldn't ever remember being so horny on a constant basis, even though like all S-species males he had a strong sex drive. He gazed at her and said softly, "I promise in a few minutes losing a game will mean absolutely nothing."

There was a flare of response in those gorgeous eyes, just as he'd known there would be. As eager as he and Trey were for sex, except for that first time, she'd been every bit as willing and even initiated it now and then.

"There's no need,' she said coolly.

But she didn't mean it. They were all starting to know each other very well for the obvious reason they were stuck together—not to mention lovers—and he could tell by the nuance in her voice she was doing her best to be the old frosty Lieutenant Thorne.

"But I insist." He stood and offered his hand.

It took about thirty seconds before she accepted it and let him pull her to her feet.

Fucking hell, I want her.

Now.

There in the common room, where at any given time they could be watched, he pulled off her shirt, exposing those perfect tits. She gave a small gasp and he wasn't sure if it was over the impetuousness of how urgent he felt or the possible exposure, but when he bent and began to suckle one very delicious nipple, she clasped his shoulders and swayed.

So warm, so soft…he licked and tasted, one hand kneading pliant flesh, the other holding her upright as he sucked her nipples to erect points.

Two weeks into their imposed stay, he knew she'd be wet fast. A body like hers was made for male enjoyment and he certainly had no complaints in that department. Larik caught her up in a swift sweep, carried her into the sleeping quarters and set her on the bed.

Don't pounce on her, he chided himself in ironic amusement, jerking down his pants as she wiggled free of hers. He climbed on top of her, used his knees to part her legs, and impatiently entered her.

Not slowly enough. She made a sound, and he froze, reminding himself she was half-human and therefore small, but when she arched, trying to take more of his length, he relaxed and eased all the way in, stretching her to accommodate his penetration.

It was embarrassingly fast, exquisitely pleasurable, and his climax shattering.

But she was left unsatisfied, he knew it, her lush body trembling beneath him.

"I'll take care of you," he whispered, still a little stunned by how she affected him. He didn't withdraw but reached between their joined bodies and began to slowly massage her clit, watching her flushed face. She made no secret that she liked it, rotating her hips, clinging to him.

When her orgasm came she cried out, her face pressed against his shoulder, her slender form shaking in his arms. In the aftermath they both lay quietly, the sound of their hard breathing filling the chamber. Though it wasn't his intention to be so candid, Larik said abruptly, "I'm not used to this."

Sprawled under him, the faint tint of sexual release still under her skin, Aspen murmured languidly, "Used to what?"

"Wanting one female so much. It's..." he searched for the right word and found it, finishing with, "powerful. I usually try and have a least a little foreplay."

She laughed, an unusual reaction for her. He found the sound stimulated him, or maybe it was just his cock deep inside her luscious pussy. No blood left in his brain—that must be it, because the word love came to mind, and he wasn't accustomed to that idea.

Maybe not love. No, that was stupid, idiotic, adolescent. Maybe possessive fit better, though he didn't mind she fucked Trey, because he knew she liked doing it. Better yet, he had a feeling that Trey might be even more involved than he was. The two of them argued on a regular basis, and she could pull off the ice queen look with York more than she did with him, but undeniable chemistry existed there. It might be the military thing, for females who advanced in the ranks had to learn early on to keep males like Trey in their place, but perhaps it was just fate.

"Obviously, *I'm* not used to it." She turned her face away, just a fraction, her profile as flawless as the rest of her. "I waited so long to have a sexual relationship because I wanted more…and…well…here I am. With you. With him."

Larik kissed her, very softly, as gentle as he had been frantic when he took her the first time. He whispered against her mouth, "More what?"

"Don't ask."

The order was tempting since he wasn't sure he was all that comfortable with the subject himself. But still, they were together, and he knew firsthand how much control it took for Trey not to come into the room. He appreciated that they'd come to an understanding that while they shared a lover, private time was important, but still he wanted to talk about the situation with her. "Aspen, come on. More means what?"

As usual, when faced with direct challenge, she didn't avoid it. Her eyes, that luminous purple shade he found so remarkable, stared up at him. "I thought I'd fall in love," she admitted. "First. It's why I waited."

Oh fuck, she'd said the word.

Larik hesitated and then admitted wryly, "It's not a concept I'm very familiar with to be honest. I saw it happen between Ran Kartel and the human who is now his wife, but it has never happened to me." He traced the delicate curve of her collarbone with the tip of his finger, marveling over how she could be both fragile and strong at the same time. "Unless that is what is going on now. Can you feel me? It's like I didn't just come."

"I feel you." Her lashes drifted shut and it was hard to tell if his comment pleased her or not. "Sex isn't the same thing as love, Larik."

She was probably right, but he could hardly philosophize over it when his throbbing cock held his complete attention. He began to move again, sliding backwards and thrusting deep, each pumping motion of his lower body making pleasure soar through his nerve-endings, flood his brain, and center lower and lower until he felt his testicles tighten, signaling the imminent rush of orgasmic release. This time, however, at least he was able to wait for her to climax first, and if the bruising grip of her hands on his shoulders and her low scream as it happened were any indication, it was both intense and satisfying. He followed, filling her with a river of sperm, his head dropping forward and a low groan coming up from deep in his chest as he ejaculated.

Afterwards he lay sprawled in relaxed satisfaction next to her, trying to still his erratic breathing. Aspen didn't seem inclined to speak either, nude and lax, the veil of her dropped lashes concealing her eyes.

He wanted to know what she was thinking.

Now that truly *was* unique in his experience.

* * * *

Trey dashed wine into his glass, mindful they had a limited supply. He glanced up as Larik wandered out of the sleeping quarters, his hair a bit disheveled. An aura of male satisfaction surrounded him like a cloak.

The engineer went and got a glass, poured the rest of the bottle of wine into it, and sat down. "She's sleeping."

"Again?" Trey felt a little surprised, but maybe he shouldn't be. In such close quarters it was impossible not hear them, and it certainly sounded like Larik might have worn her out. Aspen had taken to napping in the afternoons, but then again, they kept her in bed half the day anyway, and besides, there really wasn't much to do. She was used to activity on a constant basis, so the enforced sedentary lifestyle probably bothered her as much as it bothered him. There was a running machine, but it wasn't as effective as being able to do the same thing, and though he wasn't surprised the quarantine berth was less than luxurious, he chafed to get out.

"She fell asleep a while ago." Larik shrugged and picked up his glass to take a drink.

Trey knew that for it had gotten very quiet. What was interesting was that his companion had stayed and simply watched her sleep. He'd done that too before. Just admired her beauty in repose.

"At least if we can't really exercise any other way, we have sex." After the lighthearted joke Trey studied the liquid in his cup for a moment in abstraction. He glanced up. "Do you think Governor Kartel got your message?"

Neither one of them had mentioned to Aspen it had even been sent. They both knew she'd been ordered along to make sure military rules were followed and contacting Kartel using the Rapt One government communication system did not qualify as regulation. It did qualify as a crime, though.

"I'm sure he got it." Larik looked noncommittal. "Let's see if he does anything about it. It'll be a moral dilemma for him because he does take his responsibility seriously. If he does buy into the idea that maybe the infected visitors might have been a ploy to keep me away from the energy station, he may just use some muscle to get us out. But it's optimistic to think he'll do it without more proof. Aspen is right. It's also a stretch to think something that drastic would be done just to keep me from looking at it."

Trey agreed. He said slowly, "I've been sitting here thinking."

"Are pilots supposed to do that?"

"Very funny. Shut up, Armada and listen." Trey took a sip of wine, waited a moment, and then said, "Answer me this, why *did* they call for you?"

"What do you mean?"

He quirked a brow. "To look at the station. It seems like heavy hitting to me. You're a pretty expensive commodity and you're being sent with a military liaison. My orders were to sit on my ass here and wait until you'd figured out the problem, no matter how long it took. It was very clear. Normally I drop off transport passengers and then go pick up others. There are always transports coming and going, so the official orders to wait puzzled me at the time. It ties me up, and ties up my craft."

"It all comes back to the station, doesn't it?"

"That's my guess."

Larik surged to his feet and paced across the room. "I keep thinking that maybe we do need to talk to the Governor of Rapt One again."

"The only problem is that tricky little part about you breaking into the system. He's going to be pissed. If he finds out you used his name and code specifically to contact Minoa, he'll be even more fucking irate, I'm going to guess. If he wanted, he could have you dragged out of here in about five minutes flat, charge you with espionage, and you could even be euthanized."

Trey wasn't exaggerating. It bad enough to hack into the system, because he knew if anyone could do it and go undetected it was Larik. It was something else to admit it to a government official who had a state of emergency on his hands and a lot of power. Aspen had gone positively pale when she'd seen Armada had accessed the system on what was supposed to be a simple communication device to access galactic news and transmit generic messages.

"Kartel would never allow that."

"He isn't governor of this colony," Trey pointed out flatly. "Yes, he has influence and could probably help you, but the truth is, it could all be over before he even heard about it. Prisoners of war don't get much leniency, at a guess, even if they are someone like you. What worries me more is that if they wanted to implicate Aspen, they could charge her with dereliction of duty. She's supposed to keep you in line."

"I don't need a babysitter." It was a mutter.

Trey cocked a brow in amusement at the defensive look on his friend's face. "I think it's well known enough you view military policy as a bunch of suggestions, not rules."

"I'm a civilian." He paused by the table and picked up his glass but still stood.

"Well, she isn't and it doesn't take a genius to figure out her career is important to her. She's not only a female, but half-bred, besides being young for her rank. It's clear she's worked hard to get where she is. I think you'd better come up with an alternative plan."

"Well, shit, maybe you're right." Long fingers ruffled blond hair even further into a state of disarray in a frustrated gesture. Larik gave him a direct look, his sapphire eyes glimmering. "We're both starting to get attached to her, aren't we?"

Trey was afraid it might be true. The fascination he felt for their beautiful companion wasn't just sexual any longer. Half the time they were in bed now he spent talking to her, coaxing out details of her childhood, just touching her, sometimes even holding her hand. He liked to listen to her breathe, for God's sakes, and the way he felt a complication he didn't expect. "Yes," he admitted.

"When we get out of here it might be a bit of a problem."

"I know," Trey agreed and drank the rest of his wine in a single gulp. "In the meantime, let's worry about getting out."

"Fine. I'm open to any ideas."

"Hack back in. Let's read all the governor's communications and look at the energy station again. If you think that's the key, Armada, I'm with you."

Chapter 5

The speculative look on the faces of the rest of the council did not escape him. Ran took his seat at the table and folded his hands in front of him. Very rarely did he not know precisely what to say when addressing the most powerful body in interstellar politics, but at this moment, he wasn't sure.

Damn Armada and his cryptic messages.

He cleared his throat and began. "Recently I have received some information that might be pertinent to our current alarm over the possible attack on Rapt One. Security measures have been drastically tightened as you all know, and there is a possibility that the procedures now in place might be just exactly what the enemy wanted."

One of the elders, a statesman who had sat on the council since before Ran was born, lifted a bushy brow. "Do you mind telling me, Governor, just how *increased* security would aid whoever tried to infect the colony?"

"Well, for one, it would detain anyone coming in. The current quarantine time is two months. The question we need to ask ourselves is whether or not the virus—which was caught quickly and contained the first time because it is so virulent the victims sickened and died within a day—is the real threat."

"It depends on the incubation period. As I understand it we have scientists on almost all allied planets studying it."

"I agree the virus isn't to be dismissed lightly, but shouldn't we make sure we aren't doing exactly the expected and thereby causing a greater danger to not only Rapt One but all the colonies?"

One of the other members spoke up, a frown on his face. "Who specifically would it detain, Governor Kartel?"

"The engineer sent to repair their failing energy station, Larik Armada. He's there now, trapped in seclusion for at least four more weeks. If it is necessary to rebuild the facility, the hope is, of course, he can design it faster than anyone else. I'm sure you all know his name."

Several of the Council nodded, but none of them looked particularly convinced. Ran continued, even as he articulated the words becoming more and more certain maybe Larik was right, and his confinement deliberate. He looked around the room. "We all know terrorists often do not hesitate to sacrifice their own. It's not a covenant I understand, but it exists. How easy would it be to infect several of their members, or even innocent civilians and send them into Rapt One, knowing there would be a panic and a shut down? It's a simple plan, really. It buys time, costs almost nothing, and distracts us from the real objective."

"What's the real objective, Governor?" one of the members asked.

He'd pondered almost nothing else for the past week once he'd finally figured out what Larik really said through his infuriating code, and come to an interesting hypothesis. The Latin message roughly translated to "It's about you" and Larik had modified it in the next sentence by saying 'or in this case me.". If his old friend thought this was all about him, there had to be an important reason.

Close investigation had revealed a chilling possibility.

"The energy grid provided by the station includes several government buildings," he said slowly. "At first I wondered if they had been targeted in some way. One of them is a museum full of artifacts from when the colony was first settled. There is an entire set of administrative offices, and even a colony banking headquarters, but they all have reserve power back ups and no one has reported any suspicious activity during the series of power outages. However, I did notice something interesting when studying the map of the grid area. There's the original mantonium site in the grid. And no, it does not have a working reserve power source."

The silence following his disclosure told him they processed the implications. Finally the elder said, "I thought the mine was sealed."

"So did I," Ran agreed. "But I spent considerable time talking to every official I could locate on Rapt One who might know something about it. Since it is abandoned and the material considered useless because of its instability, they have it safeguarded by a security perimeter, but that's all. With the project such a dismal failure, the private company that ran the mine itself simply pulled out."

"You're telling us every time the power goes out anyone could have access to *mantonium*?"

Ran nodded, his face grim. "I'm saying more than that. I have evidence that the power station was designed deliberately to give opportunity for catastrophic failure at the flip of a switch. I'd guess the reason for the frequent failures and the mysterious sudden restorations is that the substance is so highly toxic and unstable if someone is secretly taking it out of the mine, they have to do so in very small amounts at a time."

One of the members, a seasoned retired soldier named Tercel with the highest rank possible ever awarded a commander, gave him a straightforward look. His mouth set in a thin, tight line. "The weapons we built with mantonium were banned because the results were so horrific the military could find no place to even test them, nor are we willing to risk any more soldiers in the attempt. Even a small amount in the wrong hands…"

He trailed off, but he didn't need to finish.

Everyone in the room understood.

"Maybe we're wrong." The one female member said it in her clear concise voice. She was also one of the youngest members, a brilliant political analyst and successful politician. Leeta Vitol folded her hands on the council table. "Where did you get this information, Governor Kartel? You said you have evidence about the power station being designed with intent to sabotage its use. All kinds of colony engineers have looked at it from what I understand."

He hesitated. If he told truth and was wrong about all of this, he could be in serious trouble. However, to give credence to his theory it was probably necessary to divulge his source. He finally said briefly, "Armada himself."

"I thought you said he was being detained in isolation on Rapt One." She looked at him with censorious scrutiny.

"He is." Ran smiled, a humorless curve of his mouth. "It takes more than being imprisoned to stop him, trust me."

* * * *

Larik heard the sound, registered what it was, and sat up so fast his head spun. Trey was already up, he saw, bare-chested, his dark hair tousled, a worried look on his face as he hovered by the door to the cleansing facility. He lifted his hand and knocked lightly on the panel. "Aspen?"

She didn't answer, probably because she couldn't.

A second day in a row when she'd woken up vomiting.

Shit, Larik thought, running a hand over his face, feeling a little sick himself but with worry, not illness. The morning before both he and Trey had refrained from saying much and by later in the day, it seemed to pass, her color came back, and she ate her late meal with them as usual and appeared normal. They had both been relieved when her daily scan came back clean. No fever, no elevated vitals, and she had finally appeared to relax, which told him she had been worried too.

Having it happen again was not a good sign. Not for someone who was in quarantine in case they'd been infected. Not for someone who was not going to be given any kind of medical care, or so they'd been told.

The sounds stopped, all was quiet from within the small cubicle, and it was clear Trey wanted to go in and help her. But just as clear was they hadn't been invited to do so. Finally they heard water running, and a few minutes later the door lifted.

She didn't look just pale, she looked positively green.

Trey immediately lifted her in his arms, cradling her against his chest. "You're going back to bed."

The lack of protest over his authoritative tone was not a good sign, and she rested limply against him, her long silky hair falling over his arm like spilled ink. He took her to the main bed, not her bunk, and laid her down as if she might break, brushing a dark curl off her cheek. Larik saw his long fingers tremble and felt exactly the same way.

Petrified.

Luckily, in moments she fell fast asleep again. In retrospect, she'd been sleeping a lot lately, but they'd both attributed it to how they kept her in bed quite a bit anyway, and there really was not much else to do.

In tacit agreement, they went into the main room. Trey didn't hide his worry, his good-looking face taut. "What are we going to do?"

"The governor said no medical care." Larik felt helpless and didn't like it.

"You saw her, she's sick, Armada."

"I know."

"Get on that fucking communications system and pretend you're the governor and order a doctor for her."

If it's the virus, no one can help her. Larik didn't want to say it out loud, but he'd spent hours going over the communiqués on what put them where they were now, trying to understand every aspect of the situation. The virus could be a replica of a rare earth strain, obliterated thousands of years ago, and was incurable. Few survived it and there was no treatment. Trying to stay calm and think, he said, "You and I both know any physician is going to question being ordered into the quarantine holding area. There's no way I could pull it off. Then they'd know two things. I can access any information I want, and that she's ill. I sure as hell don't want them to know the first, and not sure about the second. What about the med kit?"

A muscle in Trey's jaw flexed and his crystalline eyes glittered. "The standard stuff is geared to injuries more than illness, that's all."

"Fuck."

"Yeah, fuck."

They just stood there looking at each other. Trey finally said it. "If anything happens to her—"

"Don't," Larik interrupted savagely, not able to handle the idea of it. That Aspen with her vibrant beauty, cool poise, and inner sensuality could possibly die was inconceivable. Normally he could think pretty sensibly under any circumstances, but the ability eluded him at the moment. He struggled to collect his thoughts and order them in the usual way. "This isn't like the virus."

"Serious attacks of vomiting. I thought you told me that."

Think. Concentrate.

A mental inventory of the symptoms ran through his head. "Yes, true, but she didn't have a fever yesterday. No elevated white cells. Just the vomiting. She felt fine later, not worse." The more he thought about it logically, the better he felt. "No muscle weakness, no joint pain. With the virus, by the time the first symptoms appear, it's supposed to progress rapidly. If she threw up yesterday morning, she should be dead by now."

That sent Trey straight into the sleeping quarters at a run, but he returned a moment later. "Damn it, don't do that to me again or I will kick your ass. She's just sleeping."

Sleeping. A little sickness in the morning that passed. Not to mention the out of character sexual eagerness from the very beginning that neither of them had argued with one bit...a warning bell went off in his mind.

Larik suddenly felt a little weak in the knees and sank down into a chair at the table. He sat there and shoved his fingers through his hair, not sure if he wanted to laugh out loud in relief, or faint dead away. "It...well...could be something else."

Trey stared at him. "Like what?"

"I suppose she could be pregnant."

The stupefied look on his friend's face did extract a small laugh, but the more Larik thought about it, the more the symptoms fit.

Trey shook his head. "Like all female military personnel, she has a chip."

True, all females on assigned duty had a microchip implanted to keep their hormone levels such so they didn't have the inconvenience of menstruation. When and if they wanted to breed, they simply had it reprogrammed and almost immediately ovulated. It all made sense, Larik realized. Her unusual sex drive and their heightened desire for her could all be because she was in a breeding cycle. Despite all the evolution and genetic engineering, they were still basically animals in the sense males knew instinctively when a breeding female was available.

"Chips fail." He frowned. "But more likely, I'd guess, the constant medical scans could disengage it, switch it over. I believe most females have theirs checked after each exam. Here, she's having a scan every single day. I'm going to bet from that first one, she was set to be impregnated."

"Oh, hell." Trey sat down also as if his legs gave way. "Okay, that's an interesting complication to an already unusual mission. I didn't count on being a father when all was said and done."

"Could be mine." Larik cocked a brow.

"Maybe." Trey didn't blink an eye. "Either way, we'll work it out."

"I hope she isn't too upset by this. Military female personnel are required to take extended leave once they breed. The timing in her career is probably not the best."

"Yeah, good point. This is our fault essentially, not that we intended it to happen. I'm just relieved she isn't actually sick."

They obviously both were. Enough that the responsibility of child was a serious one, having Aspen be truly ill was a devastating possibility that had them both in full panic. Larik said slowly, "I'm hoping Kartel will come through and get us out of this, especially now. I want her off this planet and back on Minoa for the pregnancy. I don't like whatever is going on here."

"Any more interesting notes from Ravenot to that address you can't trace?"

Larik grinned and leaned back, folding his arms across his chest. "Who said I couldn't trace it?"

Trey lifted his dark brows a little. "You did, just yesterday. I take it that was what you were up half the night doing? I could hear you muttering away to yourself. All right, genius boy, who is the chief engineer on Rapt One sending cryptic messages to anyway?"

He sobered. "It's coded, not given a user name. That's the problem. I looked at first for something that wasn't there. The address is either pirated or stolen and reconfigured. But I can give a location when I mole back in and send my next communication to Kartel. I'm not there yet, but that's only because I can't risk staying in the system for too long."

"You're convinced Ravenot is involved?"

"I can't see how he wouldn't be. Someone built in that master switch and he oversaw every aspect of the construction of the station. If he doesn't know it's there, that means he's negligent and an idiot, and I doubt he's either. Rapt One is a prosperous colony and I'd be surprised if he could get promoted to such a prestigious position if he didn't know his job. Besides, he had to be the one to send the set of plans without the switch to both Aspen and I when we were first consulted to check on the trouble. Everything looked fine, which is why I decided to come and take a physical look at the plant. No, he's guilty as shit."

Trey rubbed his jaw, his eyes narrowed. "That means you have a built-in enemy."

That had already occurred to him more than once. Larik muttered, "Yeah, I know. What's worse, it means there someone else out there too who has a vested interest in keeping us confined as long as possible. One person does not sabotage a major power station for no good reason, and I doubt somehow he'd do it on his own. Besides, someone sent those infected visitors here to start this whole lockdown from the outside. I checked his personnel records and he hasn't left here in nearly a year for any reason. Besides, how does a colony engineer get his hands on a deadly earth strain of a disease that was wiped from the planet a hell of a long time ago?"

"We're talking treason here," Trey said with a grim note to his tone. "No recourse and no appeal if you're convicted, a three day grace period before execution. The switch being there alone might not convince the Council he plotted against the colony government, but the deliberate exposure of citizens to a virulent virus is one hell of an argument for his guilt."

"He's got a lot to lose the day we walk out of here." Larik had come to that conclusion the minute he spotted the circuit.

"Considering there have already been casualties—which means he and his conspirators are willing to kill—that makes stepping out that door pretty damned dangerous." Trey pointed at the barrier designed to keep them immune from their suspicious hosts. "If it were just the two of us, I wouldn't care so much. But Aspen is a different story. We have to protect her somehow."

He privately agreed. "She isn't going to want to be coddled, Trey. She's a military officer. If it comes down to it, she's probably the most in charge here."

"I'm in a different division entirely. I'm not under her command."

The restive words were easy to interpret. Larik said dryly, "Like hell you aren't, and I'm not talking about rank or protocol here."

"What the fuck does that mean?" His friend shot him an irritated look.

"It means I think you're in love with her. I'm damned afraid I am too, so I know the signs."

The resulting silence hung like a fading star, quiet and poignant. Finally Trey muttered, "You could be right. I don't know. I've never been possessive of a female before, but I suppose I do feel that way. It's hard to tell. We're stuck here all together. If we weren't, would it be different?"

Since the inner struggle was one he had also, Larik could sympathize, but the truth seemed pretty plain. "I was there when you met her the first time as we boarded the transport. Sorry, but the look on your face told me quite a lot."

"That's lust. I'm not going to deny it. I wanted to fuck her, but who wouldn't? Any breathing male would."

"Was it lust when you hovered outside the door earlier while she was ill? Yeah, there's nothing more attractive than a woman throwing up first thing in the morning."

"I was worried." The edge of defensiveness in his friend's voice was a little amusing.

"I know. So was I," Larik admitted, remembering the chill that touched him when he realized she was sick again.

Trey exhaled raggedly. "I get your point, Armada. But, our feelings for Aspen aside, what are we going to do about what might be happening on Rapt One? If Ravenot is doing this, and I think we established we both think so, there's a reason. What is it?"

"I'm hoping Kartel will help us out with that."

* * * *

It was astonishing how much better she felt. In fact, she was famished and Aspen ate probably more than her share of the rations provided. However, relief could be a powerful force in stimulating an appetite, she thought as she got up to clear away the remnants of their meal. A warm shower, coupled with the food and she felt perfectly fine.

Wonderful, really.

"I'm glad you're better." Trey took the serving dish from her hands, his handsome face almost carefully expressionless. "But go sit down and rest. I'll get this."

"I'm fine." She was glad beyond belief it was true. Not just for herself either, because as sick as she'd been the past two mornings, the first thing that occurred to her was if she was infected, she could have passed it to Trey and Larik.

No. Her mind starkly rejected that thought. The idea of either of them, so vital and healthy, being ill, made everything so much worse. It was a bit of a challenge to acknowledge she felt so strongly, but it was clear she did. Yes, she knew they both were attracted to her in a sexual way, but then again, she was the only available female to either of them. She'd be a fool to confuse their physical needs with something deeper.

Wouldn't she?

Yes, she would.

They were both basically decent, intelligent males, so their solicitude wasn't unexpected under the circumstances, but making their forced cohabitation into something more was some kind of idiotic female fantasy. She should count her blessings they took care to make sure she enjoyed every second of sexual play, and leave it at that. Regulation 051 did not translate to romance.

Larik lounged at the table, his face uncharacteristically somber. Usually he had a hint of that mischievous sense of humor that was so much a part of him in evidence in either the brilliance of his eyes or the set of his mouth. Instead he seemed to *watch* her.

She carried a glass of wine back to the table with her and to her surprise he leaned forward and took it gently from her hand. "Water might be a better choice."

Aspen could not help but be a little irritated at the presumption of the act, even if he did have that peculiar look of concern on his face. "I'm not sick, Armada, don't worry. I feel fine now. It must have been just a passing thing."

"Lieutenant, can you explain to me how you could catch a 'passing thing' when you're in quarantine?"

No, she couldn't, and it bothered her, but in her relief to feel normal again she didn't care to analyze the situation too much. "No, but obviously that must be it. Besides a little nausea, I don't have other symptoms. My scan is clean."

"What about the fatigue?" Trey sat back down.

For whatever reason, he too looked at her very intently.

Something was going on. If it had been anyone but the two of them, she'd guess they were worried about their personal health. But it couldn't be that. Just before dinner, both of them had kissed her; long, lingering kisses of sensual promise.

Surely she couldn't be sick if those devastatingly hot, wicked kisses had aroused her. If they thought she really was sick also, it seemed a strange thing to do.

She looked from one to the other. "I've been a bit tired, I admit that. Can I point out though that I've never been cooped up in a space this small for this long? Even on board ship there's an exercise arena and we do training drills."

Larik cocked a brow in a familiar impudent mannerism. "You bored, Aspen? If so, shame on us."

Trey chuckled softly. "Yeah, shame on us. Here I thought we kept you pretty busy."

"Are your breasts tender?"

She couldn't help it, she stared at Larik. "What?"

"I'm curious. Are they?"

"That's a pretty personal question."

"Well hell, I think about your breasts quite a bit, so humor me. For that matter, I touch them on a daily basis, so I've become a little possessive over their welfare. Just answer the question. I promise it has a purpose."

The teasing words were belied by the edge she could hear in his voice and the first real flicker of consternation stirred in her stomach. He was right there. Larik Armada might be a bit irreverent, a dash on the arrogant side, and his intelligence undisputed, but he rarely did anything without a purpose, his flippant comment aside.

And he was right. She'd noticed a little soreness but it had been the least of her worries. "Maybe."

Her non-answer seemed answer enough. "Thought so. What else have you noticed?"

The bewildering turn of the conversation had her off balance. "What else have I noticed about what? Mind telling me where this is heading?"

Trey leaned back in his chair, all lounging, careless male. He drawled, "I love her commander voice. She must have inherited that from her father."

Larik gazed at her with those gorgeous blue eyes. "I love everything about her and the fact she might be pregnant is sexy as hell."

Aspen felt momentarily frozen, trying to process what he'd just said.

"Think about it," he encouraged and took a drink from *her* glass of wine.

How he plucked it out of her hand took on a new significance.

"I can't be," she protested weakly, her mind reeling with this new possibility. "My chip is programmed against it."

Trey said succinctly, "The scans."

Oh shit, it was true. Medical scans often required the chip be updated afterwards because they deactivated the imbedded code.

If that had happened...well, it would be no surprise if she was pregnant. It would be a miracle, she realized as she absorbed the life-changing implications, if she wasn't. She'd had sexual intercourse frequently and with two virile males. Her hand went to her stomach in an involuntary movement. Her fingers splayed against the still flat plane of her abdomen and she swallowed convulsively.

"Aspen?"

Both of them looked at her and she shook her head. "I don't believe this."

"Don't believe it in a good way or a bad one?" Trey as always looked like the confident pilot with a hint of swagger in the very way he sat in his char, but there was an uncertainty in his eyes.

The answer eluded her.

Her tongue felt clumsy in her mouth. "I don't know."

"We're happy,' Larik offered. "Once paternity is established whichever of us holds the responsibility will consider themselves lucky. We both want you to know that. However it falls there's no issue there."

"I'm hoping it's mine." Trey smiled at her.

"So am I, so see?" Larik gave her a wicked wink.

A baby?

This trip to Rapt One was certainly an adventure.

Chapter 6

Governor Halden looked harried and unhappy. There were telltale dark circles under his eyes, visible even on a screen call. "Do you have any idea what time it is?"

"Yes, I do. Luckily my wife is understanding about the demands of my job." One brief call to Jerra had been their only contact all day and he missed her, but the Rapt One situation weighed heavily on Ran's mind.

"Why don't you tell me what this emergency discussion is about and maybe you can get home to see her."

Ran tapped a finger on his desk and frowned. "I've spoken to the Universal Council about the possibility of mantonium theft being behind the power grid failures. Though no official decision has been reached, it seems only fair to keep you informed on our deliberations. We're using every avenue possible to monitor known terrorist activity and assess the threat potential."

"Mantonium theft?" Halden stared into the monitor. "It's not possible. The mine is secured."

"Not when the power goes down, Governor." Ran hesitated because he wasn't interested in implicating Larik in how he'd drawn his conclusions. However, the Council already knew, so maybe it was prudent to just tell the truth and hopefully Halden would feel gratitude rather than be outraged at Armada's audacity. "I'm told there's a circuit in the design of the station to allow for failures at the touch of a switch. If you think about it, the whole thing makes sense. The station loses function for short time periods and then suddenly the system goes back up."

"You don't have to tell me that, Governor Kartel." The other man shook his head, a grim look on his face. "The problem is a nuisance, but a big one. It's why I asked for Larik Armada to be hired and sent to look at the station. The expense seemed worth it as none of the colony's staff engineers can give me an answer. However, I am at loss as to how you—from Minoa, no less—can explain this circuit theory and even offer a reason why it's happening."

"Well," Ran said in a mild tone, "it isn't my theory. It's Armada's."

"I'm sorry. It's late and I had meetings all day, so I may not be as sharp as usual. Did you say this is Armada's theory? I don't understand. He's locked in isolation along with York and Lieutenant Thorne."

"Isolation to Armada is a relative thing, sir. There's a communication monitor in their quarters."

"It's on an emergency and news frequency only. They can't communicate out."

"Can't they?" Ran gave a small cough of laughter. "Don't underestimate him."

"He breached security?" Irritation colored the crisp question.

"All in a good cause. Let's discuss mantonium. You do realize your chief engineer has been communicating with a stolen identity address, sending messages from his office. I've been waiting for something a little more concrete before I communicated with you just what's going on, but I feel as if a bomb is ticking somewhere. Which it might be, in a very literal sense. Armada says the address is off-planet. That means you might have a threat from within and without."

"Ravenot is involved?" The governor of Rapt One shook his head. "He's a good man."

"Good men have been bought before. Look, sir, one of the things you need to ask yourself right now is what good could come of anyone using subversive means to obtain an outlawed unstable element. To me it's clear the answer is none. Whether you want my advice or not, I'm about to give it. First of all, let Armada out. He's been there for a month, shows no sign of infection, and he can help in an invaluable way. Second, secure the mine perimeter with physical guards. Third, I'd monitor all communications between Ravenot and his cohorts. It's likely he's been in on this since the beginning since the actual design of the power station is deliberately flawed. Terrorists can do frightening damage. I don't have to tell you that. If they infected their own members to make sure you locked up Armada, who knows what they could be capable of. Mantonium is volatile and deadly. If there is an organization out there that has developed the necessary technique to make use of it, we're all in trouble."

Silence. Governor Halden appeared to be thinking and Ran didn't want to press too hard. The last message from Larik had been a little more urgent than the others. He really didn't blame him because being trapped for that amount of time—especially with a potentially disastrous situation brewing—would chafe.

Finally, Halden said, "I can't arrest Ravenot without some sort of proof."

Ran felt a wash of relief. "Let Armada get it for you."

"*He's* the one who I could arrest without impunity. The only way he could contact you, Kartel, is by violating about a dozen security laws."

"I admit Armada has a somewhat casual approach to protocol. But take my word, he's brilliant and trustworthy."

Grimly, the other man responded, "I hope to hell you're right."

* * * *

Aspen straddled his hips, a playful look on her face, her eyes half-closed. "Don't move, Pilot."

Insatiable was the word that came to mind as he relaxed back against the pillows propped behind him. Maybe it was the elevated hormone levels from her pregnancy but she seemed more interested in sex than ever.

Fine with him. More than fine. Paradise. Heaven.

Slender fingers wrapped around his erection and she wiggled forward just enough. Luscious full breasts, veined lightly with blue under the translucent skin, swayed as she rose, adjusted the tip of his cock at her opening, and sank down.

Yeah, exactly right. Trey shut his eyes and let the sensation wash over him as her wet heat gave to the penetration.

The woman astride him tossed back her ebony hair and gave a low telling moan as she sheathed him deep. Two small hands rested on his chest and she rocked in carnal abandon, rubbing her clit against the base of his penis.

His hands went to her hips, helping, guiding, supporting. "Oh shit, that's good. Yeah, babe, just exactly like that."

Her eyes opened and she stopped moving for a moment, her mouth tightening. "Save your flippant endearments for the awestruck little females who fawn all over you just because you're a military pilot."

He did have the ability to get under her skin and couldn't resist teasing her. Trey lifted a brow. "We're going to have a fight now? With my dick all the way inside you?"

"I'm a lieutenant, not a babe."

What she was in reality was the sexiest female alive, and how she could pull off that icy air when her naked body was flushed in arousal and her pussy holding him deep was nothing short of impressive. Trey splayed his hands across her open thighs and with one thumb, began to massage just the right spot. "All right, truce.

I'll keep the pet names limited to something you approve of, okay? How about sugar?"

"Very funny." Her voice sounded a little muffled.

"Sweetcheeks?" His fingertip circled her clitoris with subtle pressure.

"You can be irritating as hell, you know that." Her violet eyes flashed but she looked more distracted than annoyed.

In one smooth athletic move he rolled them both over suddenly, making her gasp. "You know what else I can be? Obsessed by one very beautiful, very hot, very touchy military officer, that's what. So much that I think about her pretty much every waking second."

He began to move in long slow thrusts, holding her gaze. Out almost to the point of complete withdrawal, and then a gliding push forward so he went in to his balls. He leaned forward and whispered in her ear, "I might even think the word love now and then."

She reacted. He could feel her body tense a little and her hands tightened on his shoulders. Trey let his mouth drift back so it brushed hers. "Just curious, *Lieutenant*. How would you feel if an irritating, cocky military pilot told you he loved you?"

In answer she kissed him, one hand threading into his hair and pulling his head down the scant distance needed. Their mouths mated and she arched into the motion of his lower body, the heated rhythm carrying a new, almost wild, urgency.

"Trey," she moaned into his mouth.

"Yeah, I know," he murmured against her lips.

Though his control was a fraying thread, he managed to hold on until she started to climax, her pussy contracting in small spasms around his thrusting cock, and he snapped and exploded, his orgasmic release obliterating everything except the red-hot rush of exquisite pleasure.

Panting, damp, breathless, neither of them said anything. Trey had to wonder if he'd made a mistake in telling her. It seemed logical to assume in bed would be a good time for that kind of confession, but females tended to analyze things differently than males.

He was the one who eventually broke the silence, still holding her against him, her warm breath fanning his chest. "No comment at all?"

"Assimilation takes a few minutes and I'm just now able to breathe."

He tangled his fingers in her silky ebony hair. "Well, you might want to consider that while I can navigate this quadrant with my eyes closed and fly just about anything with thrusters and controls, I'm in new territory here, Aspen. Have mercy and say some damn thing."

She rose up on one elbow. Arched brows lifted. "You're in new territory? Let's keep in mind I went from no sexual experience at all to an 051 situation and now it seems possible that I conceived because my chip was deprogrammed. You and Larik can walk away from all this if you want with your lives unchanged. I don't have that option. You know I have to take forced leave if I'm pregnant."

That she was didn't seem in question. She still had the morning queasiness and her gorgeous breasts were already slightly larger, the delicate blue-veining more prominent. However, he understood the career sacrifice she would have to make. Unplanned pregnancies rarely happened. He nodded. "Yes, I know. It was a shock for me at first too, but the way I feel about you..."

He trailed off, once again willing her to say something.

No, willing her to say what he wanted to hear.

"I won't walk away," he told her with raw honesty. "I don't even *want* to walk away."

* * * *

For an arrogant male, the man lying next to her in the rumpled bed certainly looked uncertain in a very uncharacteristic way. The hint of vulnerability in his crystal blue eyes moved her more than his whispered question during sex.

When had her life spiraled so out of control?

The answer probably was the minute she'd been assigned to this mission.

That both of them seemed pleased about potentially becoming fathers surprised her a little. Of course, if she was going to breed, she could certainly do worse than having two attractive, intelligent males as candidates. Not to mention that they were considerate, passionate lovers.

Were her feelings engaged? Yes, they were, damn them both. This was *not* how she planned her future. "I don't know how to respond," she admitted, her body languid and sated against his muscular form, but her mind restless. "I've never been romantically involved with anyone. Is how I feel normal? I have no idea. Add the child, and I'm lost as how to react to all this."

"Not exactly reciprocation, but fair enough." Trey grinned then, his signature wicked smile lighting his face. "I hate to break it to you but there is no normal, Aspen. No regulation manual you can consult on the rules over relationships, especially between males and females. From the minute I saw you, I wanted you. And in spite of the prickly manner you wear like a force shield, you weren't indifferent to me either. On my part, it's grown into more. I think you're in the same place."

"Careful, your overconfidence is resurfacing, Pilot." She gave him a cool look, belied by the fact she was in his arms, naked, with his sperm glistening on her thighs. Since he was exactly right, she didn't quite pull it off and he just laughed.

"Strong mutual attraction isn't a bad thing, Lieutenant Thorne." He shifted her more onto his chest, his fingers feathering an erotic pattern at the base of her spine. "That we feel more just makes it better. The best for me ever with any female."

Her lack of experience was the part that daunted her. "I have nothing to compare this to." She tickled his neck with her fingertips, feeling his strength and warmth.

"There's Larik."

"It's all tangled together for me."

"It's not a lot different for us."

A strange sound—or one they hadn't heard in a while—made Aspen stiffen suddenly. With a surge of both surprise and panic, she realized the door into their quarters had opened.

Since she and Trey were both naked and sprawled on the bed and the door into the common area was wide open, she gave a small cry of dismay and grabbed for the sheet. Trey dove off the side of the bed, retrieved both their sets of clothing, and handed hers over. He jerked on his pants, and then carelessly tugged his shirt over his head. "Looks like we have company."

The first stab of fear she felt as she fumbled into the issued clothing was over whether or not Larik had been caught hacking into the governmental system. He didn't say much about it— neither he nor Trey did—but she wasn't an idiot and she knew he was still stealing his way in and reading top secret files.

Trey left the room, striding into the common area. In the act of running her fingers through her disheveled hair, she heard him say, "Good morning, Governor."

It seemed inconceivable that if Rapt One had kept them isolated because they worried about contamination they'd break quarantine early by sending in the most important man on the planet. Quickly, she slipped into the cleansing facility, ran a comb swiftly through her hair and used a towel to wipe away the sexual residue before donning her clothes. Then she took a steadying breath and went out to the common room.

Sure enough, Governor Halden sat at the small table and the grim silence in the room didn't bode well. With graying hair and a stern air, he radiated authority and she reflexively saluted.

"Relax, Lieutenant Thorne, though I appreciate the courtesy. Please, sit down. We waited for you to begin."

Both Larik and Trey looked impassive, but she caught a small glint of apprehension in their eyes. Armada, she thought as she selected a chair and obediently sank into it, surely should be worried. His neck was in a noose if the governor had discovered he'd used his personal code to access government documents.

With a thin-lipped smile, Halden said, "I understand you've been quite busy, Armada. By now you probably know what color of gemstones my wife prefers."

Larik didn't blink. "Green, sir. Or at least that's what you requested last week. How was her birthday?"

Gray brows shot up at the cheeky remark. "Don't think for a minute I'm not irritated over having my personal mail accessed, not to mention your contact with Kartel in my name. We'll discuss how to upgrade our security system after we solve our other dilemma, if you don't mind."

"Not at all. You know my fee."

"I think I am beginning to understand why it is so high."

Aspen felt a wash of relief, because if the Rapt One government wanted Larik's help after the terrorist threat was dealt with, it didn't sound like an arrest for breaching code and violating security rules might be in his future. "Larik thinks he found out why the station is unreliable, sir."

"I know. So Kartel told me." The governor furrowed his brow in a fierce frown. "This issue is volatile. I need you to help me find out if mantonium is truly being heisted during the failures and more importantly, where it is going. If someone is stealing it that means it must still be on Rapt One because it is so unstable our sensors would go on full alert if someone tried to transport it through any of our air locks. They are highly sensitive to unusual radioactivity."

Trey said with solid conviction, "Armada could probably circumvent them. What makes you think no one else could?"

"I'm hoping he's unique." Halden looked dryly censorious. "I'm assured by Kartel it's pretty much the case. Either way, we've managed to track all the outgoing transports from Rapt One in the past weeks and nothing is at all suspicious. Whatever is going on it's happening here in my opinion."

Aspen felt another frisson of apprehension. "Mantonium was considered for making bombardment weaponry because of its lightweight and high density explosive properties, correct? I remember my father talking about it a few years ago. The program was discarded."

The governor nodded. "Yes, Lieutenant, that's right. The substance is too unstable. I can't give details of something that's considered confidential at the highest level, but there were accidents."

Larik shook his head, a lock of blond hair falling over his brow. "In other words, people died. So, what we have is someone—an organization hostile to the current S-species government—who thinks they can do better. Any guess as to who it might be? This keeps sounding worse and worse to me. Who would have a better capability than our own scientists and military in harnessing a substance like mantonium?"

"I can't say." Halden looked at each of them in turn. "The Universal Council has a few ideas and I doubt if even I am privy to all of them. What we need from you is Ravenot cut and dried. Prove he's in and his arrest could start the avalanche to bring the enemy to his knees. I'm not convinced of his guilt in any way, but Kartel says you insist it must be so."

Aspen spoke up. "Either he's a very poor choice for chief engineer, or he must be involved."

"Your conviction is moving, Lieutenant, but please obtain some real evidence besides the extra circuit I'm told exists."

"Oh, it exists." Larik leaned forward suddenly, his handsome face intent. "Tell me one thing, sir, have you ever heard of The Covenant?"

A slight flicker of something showed in the older man's eyes. "I'm not here to answer questions, Armada. If there's something I need to know on the other hand, I didn't walk into a quarantine area lightly. Talk to me."

Broad shoulders shrugged, and because Aspen had gotten to know Larik well in the past weeks—not just in a sexual way—she recognized the irreverent twitch to his lips. Whatever the governor wanted, at a guess, Larik either already knew it or was sure he could get it.

He said with nonchalance, "When you did his background check, sir, did you discover Ravenot was from Acadien?"

Silence. Then Halden said between his teeth, "No. And how you...oh, well, forget it, I'm not even going ask you how you found that out, Armada. Isn't he too young? The colony was dissolved years ago."

"Not too young at all, sir. He was there until he was seven. That's long enough."

Trey glanced at Aspen, his expression a mirror of her own puzzlement, then back at the governor. "If you'll excuse me, what the hell is Acadien?"

The older man looked grim, standing abruptly. "It's a classified subject, but since apparently that word means nothing to your friend, York, ask him. For my part, I am going to see you're all three given standard issue Rapt One military uniforms, arrange so you have independent transportation and weapons, and do as

Governor Kartel requested and use you to help solve this problem. Need I say the sooner the better?"

Before any of them could answer, he strode from the room.

Chapter 7

The place was one of those quiet dark places he preferred, jeweled lighting by the tables the only illumination. Soft music, modern and understated, played, and when they sat down at the elegant table, Larik arched a brow in Aspen's direction. "Since the Rapt One government is buying, this seemed a good choice."

"Something other than rations sounds good to me." Trey gave a small laugh. "I still can't believe we're out of our quarters early. Not arguing it, don't get me wrong, but it feels a bit surreal."

Aspen, once again looking like the cool, professional soldier in a black and gold tunic, her gleaming raven hair coiled neatly at her nape, said dryly, "And here I was convinced Larik's activities were going to get us in more trouble, not less. I think you owe a lot to Ran Kartel."

She was probably right. Larik nodded, not saying anything more as they studied the illuminated menu and made their choices. The drinks arrived and Aspen gave them each an ironic look as her innocuous beverage was set down. "When I think about the inequity in how we breed, I have to wonder if we are as advanced as our civilization thinks. Why is it males just experience a moment of pleasure, and females endure months of symptoms, restrictions in diet, and at the end of it all, I'm told, considerable discomfort."

If she indeed was gestating, it was still too early for her to have to go on official leave, which Larik couldn't decide if he was happy about or not. On the one hand, he wanted to protect her. On the other, she was intelligent and well-trained and could handle a weapon better than either him or York.

If they were unofficially assigned to do this, they needed her.

"Whatever the limitations," he told her with sincerity, "the condition agrees with you. I am not sure how it's possible but you're more beautiful than ever."

Luminous violet eyes looked at him and her soft mouth quirked. "Be sure and tell me that in a few months."

"It's true." Trey backed him up, his long fingers idly toying with the stem of his glass. "And I agree with Larik, I'm not sure how it's possible. Not to mention I'd never thought about breeding before this, but it's sexy as hell you carry my baby."

"Or mine." Larik wasn't precisely jealous because he was well-aware of how Trey felt about her, but he agreed in that he wanted the child to be his with a surprising intensity.

"We'll know soon enough." Aspen took a small sip from her glass, dismissing the issue. It was very hard to tell if she favored him or Trey more, and at a guess, she didn't know either.

But if there was one thing about the alluring Lieutenant Thorne, it was she wasn't just a gorgeous female but had a very well-functioning brain. She looked at them both, the iridescent lighting playing over her lovely face in lavender and gold shadows. She said, "What we need to do now is decide how to proceed. For one thing, I think Larik needs to explain whatever Acadien is and how it pertains to Ravenot and the current problem of possible mantonium theft."

"I wouldn't mind knowing also why when you asked about The Covenant the governor had such a reaction." Trey regarded him over the rim of his glass.

Fair enough. Larik wasn't military and had no interest in doing real battle with what he knew to be a ruthless enemy. His specialty was deduction and gathering mechanical data, making sense of it, and fixing problems. Terrorist wars were for those trained to deal with such issues.

"All right," he began. "I'll brief you on what I uncovered. We'll go from there on what to do next."

"This is far more my domain." Aspen looked at him with cool authority.

"I'm not arguing that. Want me to go on?"

"Please."

He obeyed the curt order, knowing she chafed a little under the indisputable fact her military career was about to be severely curtailed. Leaning forward and keeping his voice low though their table was pretty secluded, he explained, "First let's talk about the Acadien Experiment. It was a brilliant idea in a lot of ways, but like many idealistic plans, it fell short when it failed to take some variables into account, in this case, S-species nature. What happened—and this is a brief summary—is our government decided to take orphaned children and give them a colony of their own. There they'd be trained in every avenue of military expertise on the highest level, their entire lives focused on serving Universal rule. Since they were wards of the government anyway, dependent on UC support, it made sense to ensure they would grow into adults who could give back to the society that raised them."

Trey's light blue eyes glittered in the low lighting. "Okay, makes sense to me. What happened?"

"Well, one of the troubles with having a highly-trained, contained and isolated group of young men and women who concentrate solely on aggressive behavior is that it works a little too well. From birth sometimes, these individuals were taught how to fight, how to infiltrate, how to plan, how to subvert retaliation. They were supposed to do it for us, but one of the things that started to happen was natural leaders emerged, like with any military force. Throw in one or two with big ideas and a natural thirst for power and there's trouble. Different factions split. It became more than a military state, it became a war zone."

"They were killing each other?" Aspen looked troubled.

"Children were essentially killing each other. Naturally there were adults on the colony to supervise and do the training, but they were targeted first and wiped out. I guess the first hint something was very wrong there was that all communications stopped. When the next supply ship came in, the crew was eliminated and the vessel commandeered by a band who called themselves The Covenant."

"How come I've never heard of all this?" Trey demanded.

"The UC isn't all that anxious to broadcast their failures, you know that. No government is. They sent in personnel to restore order and I guess it wasn't easy. When it was finally under control they took the remaining children and placed them in different colonies all over the place."

"What happened to the stolen ship?"

"Good question. Luckily, it wasn't equipped with weaponry because it was a merchant vessel."

"You're telling us the most aggressive group from a planet of violent rebels escaped?" Aspen shook her head. "That's impossible. They could track them surely. Besides, they'd have to dock somewhere."

Larik lifted a brow. "Don't forget, they were trained in how to duck pursuit, how to survive on very little, how to infiltrate enemy safeguards. The Covenant just disappeared. When they didn't resurface after so much time passed, the official position changed from apprehensive to resigned and they declared a missing in space verdict and closed the file."

"How the hell do you know all this?" Trey's crystalline eyes held an amused gleam.

"The Universal Council's database can be pretty helpful. I just looked under possible subversives and did a quick scan. They've never taken The Covenant off their list of possible terrorist organizations, even with the MIS status. It caught my eye because one of Ravenot's communications was signed, CTC."

"So?"

Aspen said in slow comprehension, "Commander, The Covenant?"

She was bright. It was one of the things Larik loved about her. "What clued me off to the possibility is that the messages are sent in a code the military discarded decades ago. It took me about a minute to break it. Ravenot's a civilian, so my question was how would he know it? I know his personnel file by heart. There's no record of any service. It tipped me off to look deeper. The UC fields have pictures of the all children kept on Acadien. Going from his adult image on file, I digitally enhanced a few possibilities, aging them to right now, and one matched."

It was true, the likeness was almost perfect. When Larik had sensed the connection between Ravenot—whose real name was Ravins—it hadn't taken long at all to ascertain that he'd been part of the defunct and disastrous Acadien project.

"You discovered all this from our simple communication monitor?"

Larik looked at Aspen, not able to suppress a grin. "Well, not exactly. I used it to access the Rapt One system and then, because it's pretty sophisticated, to get into the master center of the Universal Council. Kartel's code was easy enough to guess."

She gazed back at him with unmistakable resignation. "How anyone thought I could get you to stick to the rules on this mission is a mystery to me. I'm just glad you're on our side. Why didn't you tell the governor this?"

"Because he'd arrest Ravenot, of course. It's a knee jerk reaction to knowing someone on your staff lied about just about everything, plotted to possibly to destroy your colony, and will eventually make you look like a fool."

"We need to stop him," she argued.

He leaned forward and folded his hands on the table. "He won't talk. You need to understand the level of their indoctrination. There were originally ten of them on that hijacked ship. Don't you want them all, not just Ravenot? I know I do because even if we manage to get him and some of the others escape, this type of thing is just going to happen again."

"Of course I want all of them."

"From what I've read in the messages, I think at least most of the original band are here. Two died to cause the quarantine, of course. It leaves at least eight. One is definitely off-planet. The address he's communicating with is in another system." He added after a pause. "I think it's on Minoa and that worries the hell out of me."

* * * *

Armada's undisciplined brilliance was not always an asset. Trey knew full well even a friend like Kartel would be unhappy as hell to know his personal code had been used to delve into files deemed by the council better buried than public knowledge.

But, his friend did have a point. If they were supposed to give Ravenot to the Rapt One authorities, it was probably better to make sure they rounded up the entire conspiracy. Just from what little he knew about it, mantonium didn't sound like something he wanted in the hands of rabid, indoctrinated anti-government radicals.

After waiting for so long for something other than regulation rations, none of them really ate too much and when they left they headed to their new quarters. It was a little disappointing to realize that while he and Armada had been put in together, Aspen had her own room, in this case, overlooking the serene inner lake that was the center of the main city. It disquieted him to think of her alone and he prowled through the apartment, noting they'd come up some in the estimation of the Rapt One government, probably due to Kartel. The accommodations were practically luxurious, especially for military standards. He went to the window and looked over the illuminated water. Blue light from beryl deposits thousands of feet deep gave the scene a pretty, if somewhat eerie glow. Because of power rationing, most of the buildings were dark.

"Can we trust Governor Halden that no one knows we're no longer in isolation?" He pressed his hands against the sill of the window, uneasy all of a sudden. "What about missing our scans? Surely medical personnel will figure it out."

"He never promised we'd have a lot of time." Aspen walked up next to him and stared out at the unfamiliar scene. He'll try and deflect too much interest for as long as he can. You heard him."

Her slender body was tense. Trey could see it as he glanced over, her profile in relief pure and lovely. He said slowly, "There's corruption in one of his highest ranking offices. Maybe we shouldn't stay here, in a place the Governor arranged for. I have this bad feeling."

Larik, one shoulder propped against a sleek metal wall, repeated, "Bad feeling?"

"Pilots get them all the time. It usually means trouble, trust me. Gut instinct has saved my ass more than once."

Aspen glanced at him and then at Larik. "You know, he might be right. You're the one Ravenot wanted to stop. It's reasonable to expect he'd have some sort of surveillance set up in the quarantine area. He's chief engineer, so he surely has access and capability for that."

"He did." Larik's mouth twitched. "I disabled it."

Trey shook his head, a wry smile fighting to surface. "Damn, Armada, is there nothing you can't do?"

"Fly a transport. I know next to nothing either about combat weapons. If we have to fight or escape, you two get to handle that part of it."

"Let's hope neither of us has to do anything then. In the meantime—"

The first flash was blinding. Instinctively Trey grabbed Aspen around the waist and shoved her to the floor, following to cover her smaller form with his body. The window imploded, spraying glass everywhere, showering down on them.

With the second one, the building rocked.

Fuck!

"Come on," he urged, grabbing Aspen's arm and urging her to crawl through the debris toward the doorway. "Armada?"

"Here."

Trey saw him on the floor also, but his face was bleeding and Larik shook glass out of his hair. "Didn't see that coming so soon, I've got to admit it. Mantonium or regular explosives?"

"Let's worry about getting fuck out of here first and save the analysis for later." A shard of glass ripped through his uniform and sliced into his elbow and Trey stifled a wince. "I'm open for suggestions, believe me."

It was Aspen who said, "I've stayed in military quarters like this all my life. Commanders always have a separate exit. They might expect us to know that, they might not."

"It's better than walking out the front entrance."

He levered himself up and let the laser read him, grateful the mechanism still worked and the door slid up. In the hall, he saw at once a melee of Rapt One military personnel, some of them half-dressed due to the late hour, on this level of the building almost all of them officers.

The building shook again, the noise deafening. Trey pulled Aspen out and promptly grabbed one man with an unfastened tunic and a confused look on his face. "This is General Thorne's daughter. Who's the highest ranking officer here?"

"What's going on?"

"I just told you, this is General Thorne's daughter. She's a guest of Governor Halden. Whatever is going on, she needs to talk to the highest ranking officer on this floor. Now."

The young captain looked at Aspen and maybe it was her calm, cool lieutenant expression or more likely it was her striking beauty, but he nodded. "Follow me. I'll see if I can find Colonel Pearce for you."

* * * *

Three tall males dwarfed her in size and she was sandwiched in the middle. Colonel Pearce, who the half-dressed soldier Trey had commandeered introduced them to, led the way, weapon drawn like hers. Aspen had felt it only fair to tell him in a few terse words what might wait as they emerged from the besieged building. "Possible terrorist attack."

"So it's true?" He was another true S-species male, with vivid green eyes and auburn hair, a decade older than any of them, with a brusque demeanor and a welcome air of tough competency. "There've been rumors building over the past month but no one is leaking much information. Apparently our high alert status hasn't helped."

The corridor was long and dark, only the occasional flicker of the failing lighting system helping them stumble through it. It led downward steeply and during the moments when the light was obliterated she felt a claustrophobic panic rise that she had to force down.

First and foremost, she was a soldier, trained to keep her nerve in just this type of situation.

Wasn't she?

No, she admitted, feeling her way along the wall in pitch blackness. First she was a female and a breeding one, at that. Now that she'd become accustomed to the idea of a life growing inside her, the perspective she'd always held on life had changed.

Drastically.

It wasn't until the walls began to glow blue she truly understood exactly where they were. At least it provided illumination but the idea of the tons of water above their head made her take in a deep breath.

"We're under the fucking lake?" Trey, who spent his time flying across galaxies, sounded almost comically horrified. If she had been capable of a laugh, she would have, but she felt a little too much the same way.

Ahead of them, the colonel nodded. "We'll emerge on the opposite side."

Behind her, Aspen heard Larik ask in his typical way, "I think I read about this project. The beryl is difficult as hell to penetrate. I'm trying to remember the logistics of it, but—"

"Armada, take off your engineering hat for a damned minute, will you?" Trey sounded strained. "Does anyone know what we're going to do when we get—and I can't wait, believe me—to the other side? How many people know about this? Who's to say they won't be waiting for us there?"

"There's a secured building." Pearce looked unworried, if a bit strange with flickering cobalt light playing over his face. "And I'm sorry, Armada, there's no way anyone could have read about it. The project was classified."

Trey gave a grim laugh. "Colonel, maybe someday I'll explain how naïve that statement is when it comes to our friend here, that is if we live through this. How far is it to that damned building anyway?"

"It's a ways."

"That's the official distance?"

Finally there was a crack in Pearce's formal demeanor and he chuckled. "Yes, it is. It's hard to gauge distance in the tunnel anyway and without light, practically impossible."

It seemed like an eternity but the passage slowly sloped upward and they finally came to a set of doors. A glowing light above one was red, and Pearce stopped dead. He muttered, "One of the hatches is down. That's not a good sign, because I'm in charge of security when we do maintenance and it was in perfect working order just a few days ago. They have independent contained power sources for just this kind of emergency. Even without regular power sources they can run for at least a while."

"Is it safe to use the other one?" Larik frowned.

"It's that or stay here."

Trey spoke up, "I'll go first, no problem. The one thing I'm *not* doing is staying here."

Colonel Pearce shook his head. "I'll go first, Pilot. There are guards posted above and I'll need to scan us through. I recommend weapons drawn. I'm not precisely sure what's going on, but from what little you told me, I don't like the hatch being dysfunctional. The timing seems too coincidental."

Unfortunately, Aspen couldn't agree more, but when Trey stepped in front of her, she caught his arm. "How much weapons training did you do?"

She knew the answer as well as he did. Pilots had to only take a basic course, while she'd had to take extensive and highly competitive instruction, especially before her last promotion. He looked down into her face and hesitated.

Then he bent and kissed her. Hard. In contrast his fingers gently touched her cheek.

Afterward he stepped back and let her follow the colonel into the hatch

The ride up was swift, smooth, and noiseless. Though she'd been prepared in every way possible, Aspen had never dealt with an actual combat situation and this one—with an unknown enemy—was more difficult than most. Adrenalin made her mouth a little dry, but otherwise she felt simply anxious to see what might be going on.

They stopped and the colonel moved to let the optical scan beam flash, the brief blink followed by the lift of the door.

Silence and darkness.

Colonel Pearce stepped forward cautiously. He murmured, "There's emergency power back up, naturally, so I don't—"

The brief flare came to his left and the hit caught him in the abdomen. He fell with a heavy sickening thud, his weapon clattering to the floor. Still in the open hatch, Aspen swore under her breath, not able to see much except maybe some shadowy forms. She fired, doing her best to calculate where the attack had come from, but there was no return fire, just ominous silence.

They were trapped. If they went back down, they didn't have the ability to scan themselves out of the tunnel on the other side. If they stepped out of the shelter of the open hatch, they were easy targets.

"Now what?" Trey asked through his teeth. "This isn't exactly ideal."

"It would be helpful if we knew exactly where we are." Larik didn't have a trace of his usual nonchalant casualness in his tone. "Cutting out all the power was smart because we don't even know where the exit to the building is. For that matter, we don't know if we could open it either. The problem with high tech security buildings is sometimes it's as hard to get out as it is to get in."

"They have every advantage, and they know it," Aspen said, the grim reality of situation making her stomach clench and a thin film of perspiration prickle her skin. She also felt a little queasy, which was unwelcome at the moment. "The real question is how did *they* get in?"

"Ravenot," Larik supplied, an ironic note in his tone. "He's been pretty busy while we were locked away."

Sprawled on the floor just a few—very dangerous—feet away, Pearce twitched and groaned.

"He needs help."

Trey caught her arm. "Don't you dare think about stepping a foot out of here, Aspen. You couldn't move him if you tried. Look, I'll do it. You open fire and cover me. If we want to get out of here, I think we need the colonel. Armada, help me drag him in."

The idea of either of them in the line of fire terrified her but she nodded. Trey glanced at Larik behind him, gave a curt jerk of his head, and dove out. She leaned across the doorway and began to fire, praying for the best.

Chapter 8

The beep woke him and Ran thrust up on one elbow and blinked. The communicator sat on the small table by the side of the bed and he reached for it.

"Kartel."

"We have explosions on Rapt One, Ran."

He'd recognized Ian Helm's signal before he answered. They were old friends and formality only existed between them in public. Helm, as a top ranking officer with high military clearance, was in charge of outlying colony surveillance. "Tell me what you know."

"Three small explosions first. Heat sensors show combat activity in what should be a restricted sector, and communications are down."

The tension in Ian's voice came through clearly. "What do you hear from Governor Halden?"

"Nothing. Like I said, for whatever reason, governmental lines aren't responding."

"That has a grim ring to it." Ran tried to think, to not feel the bite of panic. Next to him, his wife, Jerra, stirred and rolled over, coming awake. Beautifully disheveled and nude, she sat up and shook back her hair, listening.

"Mind telling me if you know what's going on?" Ian said in his normal, calm tone. "Isn't Armada on Rapt One right now?"

"Larik is there," Ran confirmed, since that wasn't classified information. "As far as the explosion goes, I have no idea."

Jerra's mouth parted and she looked alarmed, her pale hair tumbled around her slender shoulders. She whispered, "Larik?"

He attempted a reassuring smile that probably didn't work.

Explosions. Mantonium.

Well, shit.

Ian said in a cool, business-like voice, "As governor of Minoa, I respect you and your authority, you know it. As a member of the Universal Council, you have a lot of power and I would take an order from you without hesitation. As friend, however, I say bullshit. If there's trouble on Rapt One, and rumors *have* been surfacing about mantonium theft, you'd know it, Ran. Look, I want to know how to deploy help from the nearby bases, but I need information on how they should go in. What are they facing anyway? Come on, help me."

"I don't know anything for sure." Ran thrust his fingers through his hair, the possible scenarios spinning out in his mind, none of them very reassuring. "The Council is aware of a problem, but—"

"You're going to tie my hands with that damned close-mouthed authoritarian red tape." A frustrated breath echoed out. "Look, fine, you can't say what you think is exactly going on, but tell me this, are the explosions deliberate?"

"I'd guess they are."

"Big casualties?"

"Probably. If not already, there might be." Ran swung out of bed and walked over to grab a tunic and pants. "I'm going to call an emergency meeting of the Council, Ian. I'll get right back in touch as soon as possible."

He set aside the communicator and started to dress. Jerra stared at him from across the darkened room. "You can't tell me either what's going on, can you?"

"No." He fastened his tunic and reached for his boots.

"Does this have something to do with that quotation you wanted me to translate?"

"My love, I'm not sure. Larik is there, Larik sent the quote, and now there is trouble. I know only a little more myself."

Beautiful and voluptuous in the gilded light from the two moons hanging low in the distance, visible through the long windows by the bed, she stared at him with open concern. "Will Minoa have to become involved?"

Ran pulled on his boots and went over to give her a swift kiss. "I'll be back as soon as I can."

* * * *

Larik bent over the prostrate man and both blessed and cursed the latest technology in warfare. The cutting edge weapon of choice among the S-species military was a high-powered, lightweight firearm that sent a small device containing a powerful electric charge. Upon contact, depending upon the location of the strike, it was enough to stop a man's heart. In the colonel's case, the insulation properties of his uniform was designed to diffuse the charge. It had done its job to a certain degree, but he was still stunned and the hit was direct enough Larik was amazed he'd survived.

"Hit?" Pearce managed to open his eyes for a second only. A faint burnt smell lingered around him.

"Abdomen. Higher and it would have done the job."

In the distance came the sound of yet another explosion. Trey, still breathing hard, crouched down. "Colonel, is there a way out of here besides going back into the tunnel?"

"Doors on the...north...side." Pearce's face held a gray tinge and his lips were blue. "Damn, I feel like someone slammed a transport into me."

"I'd cut off my left testicle for a transport right now. And believe me, I value my balls highly, so that's saying something." Trey's mouth twisted cynically. "Look, we can't sit here huddled in an open hatch for long. They can wait us out, easy. Somebody have a plan?"

Aspen, who'd slammed a recharging cell into her weapon, looked a little pale, but otherwise resolute. "There can't be many of them. Larik said ten. Two dead of the virus, one on Minoa somewhere, and someone is setting off the explosions, probably more than one from the sound of it. So five at the most, probably less. Four to five isn't bad odds."

Only one of them was severely injured. Larik doubted Pearce could even stand on his own.

"Take my communicator," Pearce gasped a little as he spoke. "Call for…help. Tell them…we're…trapped in Station Seven."

Larik pulled it from his belt and even before he could touch the pad, it flashed. "Incoming call," he said briefly. "This is Larik Armada. Colonel Pearce is down."

"I know. This is Ravenot."

Larik glanced at the frequency call identification and committed it to memory. Then he drawled sarcastically, "Nice of you to get in touch. Don't let me forget to thank you for that month sitting in confinement quarters."

"At least you had Lieutenant Thorne, Armada."

The mocking edge to the man's tone made Larik want to do something violent and highly illegal. "What do you want?"

"My men are waiting and I'm sure you've already figured out they can pick you off within seconds. They were stationed there to prevent any escaping high ranking officers, but lucky me, you popped out of that tunnel instead. Weapons on the floor, please, and just walk out slowly."

"So you can kill us with our cooperation? No, thanks, I'll pass."

"I actually have orders not to kill you if possible. All three of you could be useful in your own way, especially the lovely lieutenant. There is nothing more useful than holding the daughter of a prominent general hostage. Having a trained pilot at the skill level of York is always an advantage, and you could help us solve a problem or two we're having with the mantonium project. Some of the bombs are going off prematurely."

"Fuck off," Larik said with cool deliberation. "I'd never help you, the only place Trey would ever fly you is into hell, and Aspen isn't going to quietly let you take her prisoner. We know all about The Covenant and Acadien, Ravins."

There was a brief pause and then a short laugh. "You *are* resourceful, Armada. Once I found out you were talking to Kartel, I knew we had to speed things up. Maybe I should make my position more clear. Rapt One is in our hands already. In case you doubt me, I'll let you finish this conversation with someone else."

That didn't sound good and the expression on his face must have reflected it because Trey said an obscene word and shook his dark head.

"Armada, this is Governor Halden. I'd like to encourage you to surrender yourselves. Ravenot claims they've enough explosives to continue a systematic destruction of the capital city. With what has happened so far in just a short time, I am forced to believe—"

The bitterness in his voice came through clearly and the brutal way he was shut off spoke more than his words. At once Ravenot was back on. "So you see, it's best you just cooperate. It would save lives, including yours. Some heroic gesture on your part is not going to change things. We've been planning this for years. We want control, not destruction, but using the latter won't stop us if it becomes necessary."

Outside alarm signals pierced even the walls of the station, the intermittent sounds punctuated by the occasional rumble of another small explosion.

"If you don't want to kill us, why hit the military quarters first?"

"It was already planned. Your release precipitated the action. If you died, you died." His voice held a figurative shrug. "Since you didn't, let's negotiate."

They weren't in much of a position to negotiate. Larik didn't trust Rapt One's former Chief Engineer in the least, but he had an injured man and a pregnant female to protect. Aspen may not appreciate his way of thinking, but in his mind, his own child could be at risk also, not to mention his feelings for her were deeply involved.

"Contact me again in a few minutes."

Aspen stared at Larik as he disengaged the exchange. "No," she protested vehemently, her training obviously asserting itself. "Our military expressly forbids cooperation with anti-federation forces of any kind."

"Have I ever mentioned you're even more beautiful when you're spouting regulations at me, Lieutenant?" He grinned, trying to portray a nonchalance he didn't really feel. "But we need to be realistic right now. Colonel Pearce is wounded and needs attention. And let's not forget we're cornered."

Only half-conscious on the floor, the colonel gave a weak cough. "She's right. Don't do anything for me."

It was Trey who said slowly, "I've seen that look on your face before. What do you have in mind, Armada?"

"That was a very enlightening conversation in some ways. I need access to a communication center anyway and this makes it more urgent. Any thoughts, Colonel?"

"There's one in this building...of course, but..."

"Yeah, but," Trey said with emphasis. "Trying to get to it without being exterminated could be tricky. I can't believe we were able to drag the colonel back in here without getting hit. If Aspen hadn't been returning fire, we wouldn't have."

Larik frowned, thinking furiously. "Where is it?"

"Near the exit." The colonel was ashen now, his eyelids fluttering. "It controls security safeguards."

"But I bet it's directly tapped into the main system, isn't it? That'll save time." Larik really didn't need an answer, he was just musing aloud. "I really, really need to access it."

"Couldn't...coded..." Clearly Pearce was losing consciousness.

"Wait a minute." Larik had a sudden flash, trying to remember the exact configuration of the way the tunnel had been set up. "Colonel, stay with me please." He knelt by the fallen man and touched his shoulder. "You said you are in charge of security in the tunnel during maintenance, right? Is there a separate communications system down there?"

"Panel...near hatches. Also...coded, but just for..." Pearce lost the battle, his body going limp.

"I bet he meant it's like the one in quarantine, only set for simple access and other basic functions. That's all right. Time-consuming, but I know a few shortcuts after navigating the Rapt One database these past weeks." Larik nodded at Aspen who stood by the control panel. "Let's go."

"Shit," Trey muttered bitterly, "I swear I knew I was going to get stuck going back down there."

* * * *

With the city blowing up all around them, it seemed like a terrible idea to go underground in case they ended up stuck there, but Aspen trusted Larik's confidence, and the last time she checked, their options limited.

Surrender was *not* an option. If they thought holding her hostage would sway her father, they were wrong. If she was captured, she knew he'd be worried and intensely involved as much as possible in any rescue attempt, but he would never budge on negotiations. It wasn't done, and he followed protocol to the letter of the regulation.

The hatch plummeted downward and came to a halt, and thankfully, the door opened. Once their opponents realized they went back down, there was nothing to prevent them from blocking the energy source needed for them to go back up.

She shivered, not liking the idea of the dark tunnel and the very idea of being trapped…

Kneeling, she checked Colonel Pearce's pulse, finding it both weak and irregular. "Larik, hurry. The faster we get him out of here, the better."

"The faster we *all* get out of here the happier I'll be." Trey held his weapon with business-like competence and looked strained. "Hurry, Armada. I'm begging you."

"I need only a few minutes." Larik pushed the panel button and it slid up smoothly, to their mutual relief. The sound of his fingers clicking away was like some strange echoing, but welcome, music in the confines of the tunnel exit.

"How come no one else used this exit?" Aspen peered into the darkness, only a hint of luminous blue in the distance.

"Blocked at the other end would be my guess." Trey stared down at her. "By the time they realized how serious the situation is, it was too late. Ravenot…Ravins, or whatever the hell his name is, isn't an idiot. As Chief Engineer, he knows pretty much everything about Rapt One."

"That's unfortunately right." Standing by the open panel, somehow Larik was able to listen to their exchange and still work on whatever he insisted was so important they risk getting locked away. "But you know, there's one thing he's completely unaware of. Or I hope so."

"What's that?" She watched him work, amazed at how effortless it looked. He didn't even hesitate as he typed in passwords and whatever other wizardry needed to infiltrate what should be an impenetrable system.

In answer he smiled, a slow curve of his mouth visible in the dim illumination. "I'm in, and if I set it up properly, all I need to do is…this."

He clicked a key.

The lights came on.

Aspen felt her mouth part in surprise.

Trey murmured, "That's better, thanks. Now, what are you doing?"

"Restoring power, blocking the subversive communication grid, sending out distress signals to the Federation."

"Is that all?" Trey's crystalline blue eyes glimmered in relief and amusement. "With one touch of a key?"

"I noticed them setting up a failure a few days ago. I thought it might be prudent to make sure I could negate it if we needed to. I installed an emergency program." Larik's face pulled into a frown of concentration. "Now I need to get to Kartel."

Having a reliable light source was reassuring, but Aspen was still worried about Colonel Pearce. They needed a medic and she was far from one except for the basic medical training every officer was required to take. "Hurry," she said in succinct entreaty.

"I'm trying…fuck, it won't let me in…oh, wait, there we go. Minoa obviously knows something is going on because the signal is jammed with communications. Let me try this differently."

The colonel's face was pallid and beaded with sweat. "If we don't get him out of here, he's going to die," Aspen said with conviction, but she wondered how they would manage. Up above waited a terrorist ambush and the other end of the tunnel was probably blocked.

"I just need to fill Kartel in on a very valuable piece of information."

A moment later he stepped back, the panel slid shut, and he came over to help Trey lift the colonel's inert form.

"Back up?" Aspen asked.

"With the power back on, we can at least see them. It evens the odds."

"I'm all for that," Trey said as they eased back into the hatch.

At that moment came another explosion, this one so violent it knocked Aspen off her feet. Dazed for a moment, she struggled to her knees and then registered an ominous roaring sound.

"Come on." Trey's strong hand hauled her up and into the hatch. He didn't let her go but held her against him and she could feel the strong rapid pound of his heart. "Get us the hell out of here, Armada, the tunnel's flooding."

Chapter 9

"We're getting all sorts of thermal activity on Rapt One," Ian Helm said with forbidding conviction. "Every major city in the colony has had significant explosive events, especially the capital, and no answers have come to any of our communications. I believe—"

The door opened and he stopped mid-sentence. A young soldier came into the room and gave a swift perfunctory salute. "Excuse the interruption, sir, but you said if there was any development, to keep you informed."

"What is it, Captain?"

Ran certainly hoped for good news. From the minute the emergency meeting of the Council convened, the tension in the room had been palpable. Ian's report hadn't made the situation any better.

The captain said, "Their defense shields have gone back up and we're getting distress signals, sir. The power grids are reactivated and Governor Kartel is getting a repeated message on the military frequency."

"From what we've heard so far, that's impossible," Leeta Vitol said crisply.

Ian glanced at him and Ran gave him back a grim smile. "My guess is Armada. What's the message?"

"I recorded it for you, sir." The young man strode over and handed him a small reading device.

The screen said: *Not having a lot of fun at the moment by the way, but thought you should know Acadien+The Covenant=UC member. L*

He frowned and looked up, trying to remember what he could about the Acadien colony experiment. It was years ago and all he'd seen on it was some archived information on the colossal failure of the project. The Covenant was a little more familiar, but not much. It was listed as a possible terrorist organization, but he hadn't actually heard any word of activity. However, Larik did nothing without cause so if he said a connection existed and a council member was involved, it was probably true.

The other nine members looked at him expectantly. He looked back, scanning over each one and wondering which face was a mask for a traitor.

The Brigadier General, Tercel, asked into the ensuing silence, "Well? If this concerns the Rapt One situation, you are obligated by your oath as a member to tell us, Governor. There are no secrets in this room."

"Apparently there are," he said in slow, deliberate denial.

Larik, damn you, you'd better be right.

"Ian." He held out the device and Helm walked over to take it. He read the message and looked up in much the same way, his gaze skimming the seated members. Then he turned to the waiting soldier. "Captain, please go pull for me any data on the Acadien Experiment and the intelligence we have on the extremist group, The Covenant."

"Yes, sir." The captain hurried away, leaving the room in a tense silence.

He addressed the Council. "As Chief of Universal Security, my authority extends to investigating any suspicions involving high level officials, including this assembly. Considering the situation on Rapt One, I think you may all need to accept that you are detained until a determination can be made."

"Detained?" One of the elders looked outraged, the word little more than a sputter.

Tercel narrowed his eyes. "I think some clarification on why would be in order. One does not rise to a Universal Council position easily, General Helm. What does Acadien and The Covenant have to do with any of us?"

Ian said with cool certainty, "I don't know, but I am going to find out."

* * * *

It felt brutal to ruthlessly urge Colonel Pearce back to consciousness long enough for his eyes to open so they could scan out, but it was better than all of them dying—including him, so Trey stifled his remorse and helped Larik hold the man upright. Thank the stars, the hatch door opened.

Now, of course, they were right back where they'd been before, only this time he could see the illuminated interior of the station. Rows of monitors blinked with the restored power, but he doubted that would last long. Water already lapped at his feet, coming up through the hatch shaft.

"This place is too low." He gritted his teeth and looped Pearce's arm over his shoulder. "We need to get out of here."

"The doors are open." Aspen pointed with her weapon, her glossy hair disheveled and loose now, the neat, regulation hairstyle long since gone. "I think that last explosion scared off Ravenot's snipers. Plus, with the power back on, we can fight back a little better. Out in the open doesn't seem to be their way of doing things."

He couldn't help but agree. "No, it sure doesn't."

"Let's go." She stepped out before he could stop her, warily looking around. True enough, no answering fire came, no movement at all.

Good. Getting shot was never Trey's idea of a good time.

Between the two of them he and Larik got the colonel out of the building. Once outside, they all coughed in the haze of post-attack smoke, trying to figure out what direction to go. One of the planet's moons hung low in the sullen sky and it was dark, the street chaotic with panicked citizens.

The chirp startled him and Trey saw Larik reach to his belt where he'd fastened Pearce's communicator. Armada said, "If it isn't our old friend, Ravins. I'm going to guess I'm not his favorite S-species male at this moment."

Trey couldn't help it, he laughed. "I'll bet that's true. See what he wants."

"And let him pinpoint our location? Hell no. Power may be restored and help on the way, but he's probably still in control for now and I'm not interested in what plans he might have for us."

"Pearce needs medical care and we need transportation."

"I couldn't agree more."

They found both a few minutes later in the form of a military patrol that started to pass by. One look at their uniforms and the unconscious colonel, and they were all hustled on board. They shot past the draining lake, the water level leagues lower, the iridescent blue glow startling with the reduced depth. While Aspen filled in the commander in precise short phrases on the possible situation, Trey and Larik did their best to keep Pearce from being jostled, the speed of the journey necessary but not all that comfortable.

"What do you think Ravenot is doing?" Trey asked as they skirted a burning building, the destruction not complete by any means, but extensive. "The explosions seemed to have stopped."

"Waiting for orders." Larik's mouth curved in one of those signature grins. "With luck, Kartel will make sure they aren't coming. Without their driving force, The Covenant is impotent. One powerful identity can influence a lot of followers."

"Orders from the source on Minoa?" Trey guessed.

"Yes."

"Speculation or fact?"

"Oh, fact, I'd say. I have a good idea who it is, too, but the dossier of background information is as whitewashed as Ravenot's, if not more. Kartel is going to have to figure it out on his own for now."

Trey looked at Aspen, still conversing with the leader of the military team, her expression serious and all business. Yet, despite the uniform and disciplined conduct, she was also all female, slender and delicate, and he couldn't control his protective instincts. "What about us? For my part, I'd love to get the hell off Rapt One and never come back."

Larik followed the direction of his gaze. "I couldn't agree more. With Universal forces coming in, it's going to get real interesting down here. I'd rather be out of the line of fire."

Trey sent him a challenging look. "Can you get us anywhere near a transport craft?"

His companion grinned. "What do you think?"

He grinned back. "You find it, I'll fly it. We're gone."

* * * *

She was sleepy and Aspen lay back in the seat, her eyes half-closed. Outside the windows the stars flashed by, little glimmers of light that barely registered.

"You need to go to bed."

There was no argument from her, but she didn't have the energy to move. "Are we out of range?"

Strong arms slipped under her lethargic body and lifted her. Trey whispered in her ear, "On a set rendezvous for a military ship headed to Minoa. Guess how we can entertain ourselves most of the way."

How could her body stir when she was so tired? Maybe it was the sultry tone of his voice, maybe it was that Larik followed them into the sleeping quarters. The bunks were narrow and meant only for one person at a time, so she found herself on a blanket on the floor, supine as together they efficiently stripped her uniform off.

They both undressed with unhurried precision, and she could feel the answering rush of dampness in her pussy as she saw they were both erect, both ready and hard. Larik spread her legs first, lowering his head, his mouth grazing her labia, causing tingles of sensation. Trey lightly massaged her breasts, his skillful fingers working magic before he began to tease her nipples with his tongue.

Heaven. The pregnancy did interesting things to her libido and she shifted, opening her legs wider, the first climax building easily before it exploded in a shimmering cascade of pleasure. Larik kept her there, gently stimulating her clit until she came again, this time with a small scream.

"On your knees." Trey urged her up, lifted and positioned her. "Suck his cock, Aspen. I want to watch while I'm inside you."

Up until this point she'd resisted doing anything that made her feel the least subservient. Maybe the events of their tumultuous escape from Rapt One made her less resistant, maybe it was the imprisonment and their harrowing experiences in the tunnel, but she obeyed. She moved to her hands and knees, with Trey behind her and Larik on his back in front of her, his legs spread so she was between them, the stiff length of his cock jutting upward. As she leaned forward to lick the glistening crest, she felt Trey's hands at her hips as he entered her from behind.

All of him. That long length delicious stretching her throbbing saturated tissue, nudging her fertile womb. She took Larik's stiff penis in her mouth, sucking with light pressure, and saw his lashes drift down as he made a sound like a growl low in his throat.

"By the stars, yes," he said on a gasp, his thick blond hair tousled and those sapphire eyes half-closed.

Trey began to move in slow, heated thrusts and she couldn't stifle a small moan. With one hand she braced herself, with the other she stroked Larik's rigid length and fondled his testicles as she caressed him with her mouth.

They moved as one. She swayed forward as Trey thrust into her body, at the same time taking Larik's cock to the back of her throat. Then they moved in tandem backwards, a delicate erotic balance of entry and withdrawal, of taking and giving.

Larik came first, pulling free from her mouth and ejaculating so that sperm coated his broad chest, the small pulses sending a spray of gleaming liquid over the defined muscles. Trey followed almost immediately, pushing deep and going still, his fingers finding her clit and exerting just the right amount of the pressure so she shuddered in reaction and the inner clench of her muscles made him groan as she climaxed.

Sated, limp, content, she drifted afterwards, aware of her position between them. Warm, safe, protected.

A hand stroked her hair. She made the effort and lifted her lashes. "Uhm."

"You're so beautiful, Lieutenant." Larik had his habitual sexy smile in place. "I thought so even when you had a weapon in your hand, firing at the enemy."

Trey feathered his fingers down her bare arm. "I thought she was the most gorgeous when she was spouting military jargon at the commander of the patrol and helped us find this transport. I believe she impersonated a higher ranking officer."

She had in a definite violation of the rules, but when Larik had told her where a fueled transport was and Trey had promised to fly them off Rapt One, she'd been more than willing to take the risk.

"What are you two going to do, turn me in?" She gave a small, involuntary yawn. "It helped get us out of there, didn't it?"

Larik laughed. "See, I knew I could corrupt even a straight-laced, upright officer like yourself, Lieutenant Thorne. By regulation is fine, unless…well, you need to bend the rules."

"It seems to me you left behind a colony in complete chaos, Armada," she said in cool reprimand. "I'm going to guess I'll be writing reports on this for weeks to my superiors."

"Hey, I didn't cause the chaos directly and it would have happened sooner or later with or without me. I was the catalyst maybe, but The Covenant also failed."

Yes, it had. She yawned again.

"You need your rest." One of them kissed her. She thought it was Larik, but it could have been Trey, the pressure against her lips soft and gentle.

Then she drifted off.

* * * *

Ian touched the condensation on his glass with a long forefinger, his expression thoughtful. "Leeta Vitol ended up on Minoa because the Governor at the time felt guilty about the misfire of the Acadian Experiment. He took her into his family, and she was bright, ambitious, and I doubt he ever suspected in any way she was in touch with the faction that stole the cargo ship and escaped."

Ran replenished his drink. "I thought our background checks inviolate, but actually, I would never have blinked over her association with the Acadien group. You have to know the history and the tie to The Covenant. Leeta Vitol was successful and progressive in her thinking. Yes, a little aggressive now and again, but she was the only female Council member. I thought it was expected she would need to make sure she was heard."

"Everything was organized by her. The whole group answered to her direction. According to Armada, when he spoke with

Ravenot and he mentioned they knew Armada could contact you, it made them speed up their plans. That's when Armada realized it had to be a Council member. You wouldn't have told anyone else."

"Not even my wife," Ran agreed wryly.

Ian looked at him, his dark eyes serious. "They had a pretty complicated agenda planned. Starting with the outer colonies, they were going to take over one after another. With the arsenal of resources on Rapt One, they would be a formidable force. The stolen mantonium was the least of it. If they managed to rule several more planets, they might have slowly spread their power, like an infectious disease. With Vitol on the Universal Council, they would have always known what was coming next, too. Our military would have been met with precise resistance because having the upper hand is imperative in any battle. She could feed them inside information at every turn."

"You're saying it might have worked." The idea of it chilled him..

"It might have." His friend nodded, leaning back. "What are you going to do?"

"With Vitol?" It bothered him, euthanizing a colleague out his realm of experience. "The penalty for treason is clear. It was no secret to her what would happen if we found what she was doing."

"But," Ian said with unemotional logic, "this is a monster Minoa created. She was sent at birth to Acadien. What happened next isn't really her fault."

Through the large window in the dining cubicle he could see the spattering of stars across the sky over Minoa's First City. In another room Jerra sang to one of the children, her voice low and sweet. Ran rubbed his jaw as he tried to picture one of his own children abandoned and placed in an atmosphere without soft arms to hold them, no songs, but instead intense disciplined training. "I know."

"She was raised to try and seize control. To view the universe by order of who has power, who doesn't, and where it might be taken."

"The point is made." Ran restlessly reached for his glass and took a drink. He set it down. "Are you saying we should show leniency? Your observation is the very argument against her. She can't be changed. Set her free and The Covenant might form again."

"Ravenot is dead." It was true, the chief engineer had been found in a lifeless state, probably from a self-inflicted shot. Ian added gruffly, "I'd do the same thing in his place. I'd prefer to die my own way."

"It will take years for Rapt One to rebuild. We aren't even sure if we recovered all the stolen mantonium. There's no way to tell."

"True."

Ran cocked a brow and stared at his old friend. "You think we should show mercy."

"It's time the children of Acadien learned what it meant, don't you agree?" Ian stood to his impressive height in one fluid movement. "Please thank Jerra for dinner for me."

After he'd gone Ran went into their sleeping quarters. Their daughter still slept in a small cradle by the bed, peaceful and quiet, long lashes pillowed on her plump cheeks, her thumb nestled in her mouth. Jerra held an open book, tendrils of golden hair tumbled over her bared shoulders. She glanced up as he came in.

He said unnecessarily, "Ian left. He said thanks for the hospitality."

"He's always welcome here." She smiled in a quixotic curve of her soft lips. "Now, tell me what's wrong."

A short laugh escaped. "Do you know me that well?"

"Yes."

She did. She was his mate in every way and he adored her. Ran wandered over and sat on the edge of the bed. "It wasn't said in so many words, but he wants me to intervene on behalf of the captured members of The Covenant."

Jerra knitted her brow. "Does he?"

"I'm unsure if it is the best course. Vitol was a member of the Universal Council and she plotted to take over a planet with plans for further coups. It's treason, through and through."

"I see."

He shot her a rueful look. "You agree with him, don't you?"

For a moment she was quiet, and then she nodded. "I agree that Minoa is very powerful and can make a statement over this one way or the other. A handful of rebels almost took over an entire colony. It has you shaken. But the truth is, our own government trained the rebels and look how efficient they ended up being. All of them had ascended into high-ranking positions, and all of them believed in the cause of liberation. Yes, they were willing to use violence, but on the other hand, they didn't use the virus, which they could have. They didn't kill Governor Halden or his staff, and most of the explosions were set in places to cause mayhem but not kill. They wanted power and control but you must admit they had the capability to do much more damage."

"True," he admitted grudgingly.

His wife's smile was punctuated by a laugh. "You, darling, are upset because you never suspected Leeta Vitol. Your pride is injured."

Was it? Maybe. He stood and slipped off his shirt, and then sat back down to remove his boots. "Tell me more about how I'm feeling."

Her lacy lashes lowered a little. "Are we still talking about The Covenant?"

"No." He crawled into bed beside her and took her in his arms, his mouth finding hers in a searing kiss.

Epilogue

The man behind the desk folded his hands together and looked around the room. A muscle twitched in his cheek. "Shall we discuss regulation 051?"

Aspen stifled an inner sigh.

To her amusement, both Trey and Larik seemed incapable of a response. The flippant, rule-defying genius engineer and the cocky pilot silenced under a father's accusing glare. How interesting.

It was comical to see them disconcerted, but she wanted nothing more than to go home. Upon landing on Minoa, the last thing she expected was to be ordered straight to her father's office. A reunion would be nice, but an official lecture she could live without.

She said, "It was an unusual situation."

"It certainly was. As far as I can tell, you three almost managed to destroy an entire planet. Then you left without orders, not to mention commandeered property of the Rapt One government. I don't even want to get into the serious nature of the security breaches, both on Rapt One, and apparently even into the Universal Council system."

That was neither fair nor accurate—except for the part about the transport, and well, also the security infringement—but a huge argument held little appeal. "Can that be changed to we stopped an entire planet from being destroyed? Really, Father, I—"

"Luckily, I have influence and so does Governor Halden, and for some absurd reason, Governor Kartel is fond of Armada, so everyone is just going to look the other way."

She had wondered how her superiors felt about her abysmal failure to keep Larik in line when it came to military protocol, but since she was going to be on forced leave anyway, it probably didn't matter all that much. Besides, she sensed her father's disapproving glower had much more to do with her pregnancy— now quite obvious, than what happened on Rapt One. Larik was the unofficial hero of the day, even if the government wasn't interested in acknowledging it publicly because of his high-level infiltration into the databases. Technically, he should be charged with espionage.

Her father transferred that cool stare to her. "Since you are a grown woman, the physician you consulted on board the ship refused to tell me anything about your condition other than that you are healthy and everything appears normal."

"I was sick in the mornings at first," Aspen said using the same matter-of-fact tone, "but feel fine now." She had to fight the urge to place her hand on the rounded curve of her stomach.

"Your mother was the same way when she carried you." For the first time his expression softened a little. Then he compressed his mouth together and shot a lethal look at the two males sitting in upright in chairs, their usual nonchalant confidence not in evidence. "You had a genetic scan, I assume, to determine paternity."

"Yes."

"And? Which one will I have to deal with on a permanent basis?"

Both Trey and Larik looked at her. So far she had refused to reveal the results of the test, wanting to wait for the right moment. This wasn't really what she had in mind, but they all had to know sooner or later and her father was irritated enough already.

"Actually, both." She blushed, she couldn't help it. Warmth suffused her neck and cheeks.

There was a small silence. Trey said, "I'm a little confused, so maybe you can clarify for me how two males can father the same child."

"I hate to agree with you on anything, Pilot, but on this point I do." Her father frowned, his brows shooting together. "Aspen, explain, please."

"I think I can." Larik's mouth twitched into a pleased smile. "Twins. That's it, isn't it? Fraternal twins. It happens now and then when a female releases more than one egg and has multiple partners. It's rare, but there are plenty of precedents. One study several years ago stated—"

"Armada, skip the medical lecture, will you?" Trey shook his head in exasperation, but he wore the same incredulous smile. "Is there anything you *don't* know?" His expression was poignantly hopeful as he looked her. "Aspen, is it true?"

She nodded, her throat a little tight with emotion. Both of them had made it quite clear they wanted to be the father of her child and in her mind, the way it worked out was a miracle. Choosing between them was impossible. She loved Larik with his amazing intellect and quirky sense of humor, and she loved Trey equally with his teasing charm and bravado. They were considerate lovers but more importantly, decent and caring in every other way as well. Their hovering solicitude on the journey back to Minoa had driven her a little crazy, but she had also felt cherished and protected.

Her father seemed speechless, which was a rare occurrence.

Trey turned and slapped Larik on the back. "Congratulations, Armada. Excuse me a minute, I have to go kiss the mother of my child."

Larik stood also, his sapphire eyes gleaming. "Yeah, well, don't take too long about it."

Hours later, comfortably dressed in a soft robe, her hair loose, a content smile on her face, Aspen stood at the window in her sleeping chamber. The glow over the first city washed the buildings to a gleaming red and both moons hung low over the skyline. It was nice to be home, but that wasn't what prompted her serene state of happiness. Waiting for love had once been her romantic secret, a dream she wasn't sure would ever be realized.

Who could know she would be twice blessed?

Her hand moved over her stomach as she felt the flutter of life there. Twice blessed in more ways than one, she thought with a peaceful inner joy.

THE COVENANT

The Starlight Chronicles 2

THE END

WWW.ANNABELWOLFE.COM

ABOUT THE AUTHOR

Annabel Wolfe loves all forms of fiction, including fantasy worlds full of danger and sexy characters. She also writes historical erotic romance as Emma Wildes and suspense as Kate Watterson.

Please visit her at www.annabelwolfe.com, www.katewatterson.com, and www.emmawildes.com.

Siren Publishing, Inc.
www.SirenPublishing.com

Printed in the United States
209447BV00007B/24/P